Afsaneh's Moon

❧ MEHRI YALFANI ❧

McGilligan Books

National Library of Canada Cataloguing in Publication

Yalfani, Mehri
        Afsaneh's moon / Mehri Yalfani.

ISBN 1-894692-03-9

        I. Title.

PS8597.A47A64 2002   C813'.54   C2002-903489-2
PR9199.3.J25A64 2002

Editor: Rivanne Sandler
Copy editor: Noreen Shanahan
Interior Design: Heather Guylar
Cover Illustration: Shirin Mohtashami
Cover Design: Heather Guylar

McGilligan Books gratefully acknowledges the support of The Canada Council for
the Arts, the Ontario Arts Council and the Ontario Book Publisher Tax Credit for
our publishing program.

The Canada Council | Le Conseil des Arts
FOR THE ARTS | DU CANADA
SINCE 1957 | DEPUIS 1957

ONTARIO ARTS COUNCIL
CONSEIL DES ARTS DE L'ONTARIO

In memory of my uncle Reza Soudagar
who taught me the beauty of writing.

Acknowledgments

I would like to thank Marguerite Anderson, Gabrielle Monaghan, Francis Johnson for their comments and support.

Also my special thanks to Ann Decter for her editing and support and to Professor Rivanne Sandler.

It is said that one day he was talking about love. A bird flew down from the sky and sat on his head, on his hand, at his side. Then it tapped its beak on the ground until it began to bleed and collapsed.

Faridedin Attar,
Texkeratol-olia

❦ ONE ❦

You invaded my sorrowful heart
like the sudden stroke of a blade.
Charles Baudelaire

I BELIEVE EVERYTHING that happened to my family this year, happened because of Afsaneh's bad luck. I remember it was Nowruz, and her wheat and lentil seeds didn't sprout. They were rotten and she had to throw them away. She took it as a bad sign. Whenever she thought of the seeds, she said, "I'm afraid something frightening will happen to my family." She didn't really mean her family. She didn't have any family. She meant mine. She used to say my family was her family, Ramin and our son, Damon. And yes, as Afsaneh predicted, something terrible happened to her, I believe, and almost to me and my children.

Thank God, I made it home safely. What a long way! I was happy I didn't get lost. Perhaps that was because I was driving home, saving my children's lives and my own. Bahram thought I was too stupid to understand what he was thinking. I pretended to be stupid, but I wasn't as dumb as he thought. If he's fed up with life, he can kill himself. Why sacrifice us? I would die for my children; my dear Damon, my pretty Afi. Not Afi or Afsaneh anymore, now she's my Negin. Afsaneh was the name Bahram gave her. From now on I'll call her Negin. She's my Negin and he has no right to call her Afsaneh, after the woman he loved and lost. Bahram was tired of his own life, he wanted to join those two, to take my children down to her palace of genies and fairies. Too much alcohol — he didn't know what he was saying.

Last night I was scared to death. Bahram knew I was scared. He teased and mocked me as he often does now. He was never cruel at the beginning of our relationship. Back then, he was a man who fell from heaven just for me. My life changed abruptly.

My friend Mahboobeh couldn't believe it. Mahboobeh, Fataneh, even I couldn't believe it. Since I left Iran my life has been miserable, in Turkey, and here, in Canada, too. I had nothing and wanted everything. I couldn't even imagine a comfortable life. Bahram changed that, buying me a house, furniture, a car. Still, I'm not crazy enough to let him drown me, let him throw the three of us into a lake. Madman! Crazy from drinking, always drunk. In the beginning, he drank less. And then...I don't know what happened. When Afi, I mean Negin, was born, he was so happy. As if she was his own child. He stayed with me through the whole labour. Holding my hands in his. He soothed me. When the baby was born, he took her in his arms. And then at home, he fed her, changed her diapers, rocked her to sleep in his arms.

I talked to Mahboobeh about him. She said, "You've become happy." I was happy. It wasn't a trick. Fataneh said, "You won the lottery." He was better than winning the lottery, you can't win a gentleman like Bahram in a lottery. Bahram gave me money and happiness. And then...I don't know what happened. It didn't last more than a year before he changed — like someone overwhelmed. He became another person: drunk, moody, unbearable. Only kind to Afi. He couldn't bear Damon, and my poor son had done nothing.

Initially, Bahram liked Damon. He bought him expensive toys. The child squealed with joy. But later, after the change, he would send Damon away harshly, "Go to your room." The child choked back tears and came to me. I couldn't understand Bahram. He didn't treat me like a real person. He mocked me and made fun of me, made fun of the way I dressed, and my make-up. I didn't know what to do to please him. Whatever I did, he was unhappy. He wasn't like that in the beginning. He spoke as if I wasn't there, as if he was talking to someone else. Then he'd realize with surprise that I was sitting right in front of him, listening, and he'd apologize for tiring me out.

Once he said, "I have a past. I mean, I'm not an innocent, I have problems. Do you think you can live with me?"

His past, whatever it was, wasn't important to me. I was worried he would leave me. I needed him. After Ramin left, I was desperate; pregnant, and a four-year-old child. It wasn't easy. Mahboobeh comforted me, saying, "A single mother can cope here. The government helps and you can work when your children get older."

I laughed at her. I don't like to work. Housekeeping and taking care of children are all I can manage. I can do no more than that. Anyway, what kind of work could I get? I'm an Iranian immigrant with no proper education, they won't give me an office job. The best I could get would be work in a donut shop, a store, or on a factory assembly line. I'm not made for that kind of work. I've never done it. Just standing on my feet for eight hours is more than I can tolerate. I didn't give birth to two children to do that kind of work. Before I had children I worked for a few weeks in a boutique, as a clerk. The owner liked me. I was good-looking and attracted customers. But I couldn't stand it. I liked the money but I didn't like being on my feet six or seven hours a day, while my employer ordered me to do this, to do that. I arrived home dead tired. Ramin had to take care of me. He didn't dare speak loudly, or I screamed at him. Ramin told me to quit my job. Then he told me never to work again. He knew if I worked I would make his life hell. I didn't have the strength for hard work My body couldn't take it. Ramin said it was better for me to study.

Actually, we came to Canada thinking we would have a chance to finish our education. But it didn't happen. It wasn't easy to go to school and work at the same time. Even if one of us had managed a degree, nothing would have changed. Some Iranians study for four or five years in Canada, and what do they get? Take Mahboobeh and Mehdi. When we first arrived, Ramin and I stayed with them for a few weeks. They helped us a lot. I wasn't in good health, I'd just had a miscarriage. Middle of winter. How cold it was! Bitter. First we went to a shelter. We called it a "beggar's house." All I did was cry. I didn't eat, or speak. Ramin was fed up with me, but didn't dare raise his voice. He knew I'd only get worse. Ramin found Mehdi, and Mehdi came to take us to his home. When I saw him for the first time, I didn't recognize him. In Iran, he was a friend of my father's. We called him Mister Farhoodi. A civil engineer, with a grand house in Naft Street and a big swimming pool. When I was younger, I swam there. Here he seemed older, ten years older, than he was. It had only been a year since he'd left Iran. Ramin called him, "Mister Farhoodi." He laughed loudly and said, "A monster came and took Mister Farhoodi away. Here, I'm just called Mehdi. Everybody is called by his or her first name here, even the Prime Minister." In Iran we had called his wife Mrs. Farhoodi, but here she was simply Mahboobeh. At that time, they both wanted to go to school. They were waiting for the government to offer them a training course. Well, they completed those courses. Mahboobeh took evening courses and got her early childcare education certificate. In Iran, she was a physics teacher, in high school. Here, she wanted to do early childcare. What happened? Mahboobeh works part-time in a daycare. She's been laid off three times. Mehdi worked for the government in computer graphics. He too was laid off at the beginning of the recession and went back to his first job, driving a taxi he called Rakhsh, after the horse of the mythical Persian hero Rostam. He says he has his own Rakhsh. Recently he bought his own taxi and works for himself. They act as if they are happy. They're happy for their children, who have a chance to be educated, to become engineers or doctors. But their younger son doesn't do well in school. He wears an earring and dyes his hair.

When I see these educated people, I say to myself, what's the use of education? If I studied and had a job, I would always worry about losing it, like Mahboobeh is. And if I didn't have a job, then what's the difference? Life plays tricks on you. Who could imagine that a man like Bahram would appear in my life? After Afsaneh stole Ramin from me and disappeared like a genie, I was desperate and vulnerable. Before that, I had been proud of myself, because I had kept Ramin from falling into Afsaneh's trap.

It was the last year we were in Iran, before my brother Siamak was jailed. Ramin had known Afsaneh for a few months. She came hiking with our group twice. He told me they were just friends. Then I found out she was from a rich family and her father's only heir. I didn't know why she chose Ramin. She wasn't bad looking, and she was tall and fit. Her mouth was a little big, but her smile was pleasing. She had been educated in France for a few years. Ramin was a first year university student, but then the universities closed. Ramin had nothing to do, and as his father said, he had no prospects.

Eight years later, when I saw her in Montreal, I couldn't believe she was the same Afsaneh. Life plays strange games. Since arriving in Canada I had almost forgotten about her. Surely Afsaneh couldn't touch Ramin anymore. I had been right, back in Iran, to hurry and marry him. Everything forced me to marry early, even though it wasn't the right time. I hadn't finished grade ten. Ramin was only twenty. Maman and Baba were worried about me. I wasn't someone the government was interested in, but many young girls and boys who were arrested and executed overnight weren't political. They could simply have sold an activist newspaper, distributed newsletters or even gone hiking with a student group. I wasn't interested in politics and didn't understand politics. I didn't participate in meetings either. My brother Siamak used to say it was too early for me. It was too early. It was hard for me to understand what they were talking about. And now I don't remember a single word. Siamak worried about me. He told Maman, Baba and Ramin to take care of me, to send me away, maybe out of Iran. Then I noticed Ramin was interested in Afsaneh. On one of our group hikes, I realized they weren't just friends. I'm a woman and very quick about such things. I had to keep Ramin away from Afsaneh. They were close. They went hiking together during the week and out to dinner in restaurants. Years later, when Afsaneh separated from Bahram and came to stay with us for a few days, Ramin and Afsaneh reminisced about Tehran. They spoke in secret and didn't want me to hear. But I heard them talking and imagined the rest. They thought I was stupid. But I'm not. After a few days, Afsaneh went to a shelter.

The day I met Afsaneh in Montreal, I couldn't believe my eyes. We stared at each other for a moment. Ramin had Damon on his shoulders — he was standing further away, listening to the music. I was watching people. The street was full of music. It was summer. I like the summers here. People wear colourful dresses, shorts and loose blouses. The first summer was very interesting; both old and young wore shorts. Ramin said, "these people have an obsession with dressing lightly because they have to wear heavy clothes so many months of the year." I wore shorts the first year. Ramin was against it, but I didn't care. Many Iranians didn't wear shorts their first year in Canada. Mahboobeh and Mehdi made fun of Iranians wearing shorts. Now they wear shorts, too. Ramin didn't for two years. His hairy legs made him shy. When he saw legs that were worse than his, he lost his shyness.

That day, Afsaneh wore a long skirt and a pale yellow shirt which matched the flowers on her skirt. She looked very pretty. Plucked eyebrows, eyelids a shade of blue. Her hair was short, and seemed curlier. We watched each other for a few moments. She seemed familiar. Then we recognized each other. I smiled at her, automatically. She stopped walking and said, "Negar?"

I said, "Yes."

"I'm Afsaneh," she said.

"I recognized you," I said.

"How pretty you have become!" she said.

"You, too."

Ramin moved closer to us. I looked at him. He recognized Afsaneh, astounded. He didn't say anything to her, just looked at her. Afsaneh looked at Damon and said, "Your son?"

"Our son," I answered.

Afsaneh looked at me and said, "I can't believe it."

"Why?" I asked.

She looked surprised and said nothing. That day I had made myself very pretty; with blond hair and green contact lenses, I looked like a Canadian. Nobody believed I was Iranian. Damon looks like me, with a pale complexion and tiny body. But Afi, I mean Negin, looks like her Baba. Bahram says she looks like Afsaneh. Afsaneh? Isn't that funny?

Standing quietly beside me Ramin watched Afsaneh. Maybe he was tongue-tied. Afsaneh invited us to an ice cream parlor close by. Ramin had still not said anything. I accepted her invitation. She told us she had been married for two years and a few months ago she immigrated to Canada, to Montreal.

"Do you have any children?" I asked.

"Not yet," she said, and sighed – a shadow of sadness crossed over her face. The whole time we were having ice cream, she played with Damon. Damon was a shy child, still is. Now he's worse, because Bahram ignores him. He keeps to himself and complains a lot. Then, he was only two and just learning to speak. Sitting on Afsaneh's lap he quickly became comfortable with her, playing with her necklace and hair. When we went to say goodbye, Damon didn't want to leave her.

Later on, when we got to know each other better, I tried to find out why she didn't have any children. She said it was because of her husband, Bahram. Bahram told me the real reason. He talked to me about his past, about Afsaneh, Hanna, his sister Behnaz, and his childhood. I didn't like listening when he talked about Afsaneh. She was like a goddess to him. I wasn't sure whether he still loved her or not. But if he did, why did he come to me?

"You're like a defenseless child," he told me when we first met, "someone should take care of you."

I wanted someone to take care of me. I was raised that way - protected and pampered. Afsaneh was the only person who didn't take me seriously. When she separated from her husband and moved to Toronto, we developed a close relationship. She lived in a shelter for a while. Sometimes she came to our home for an evening or a weekend afternoon. I wanted to visit her at the shelter, but she said it wasn't worth seeing. Then she got an apartment, in one of those government apartment buildings. Ramin insisted we apply, too. I didn't want to. A small apartment in a dirty building, no room to breathe, with a disgusting smell in the elevators. Tenants mostly unemployed, all different races and nationalities. I couldn't live there.

Yes, our rent was high, it was a two bedroom apartment, $950 a month. It wasn't my fault. Rents were high everywhere. People paid more than we did. When I saw Afsaneh's apartment, I felt sorry for her. It wasn't comparable to her place in Tehran, a roomy apartment in upper Yousefabad, with north windows overlooking the Darakeh Mountains. The south windows opened on the tall trees lining Yousefabad Avenue with its flowing creek. She had fancy furniture and beautiful paintings on the walls. A fine green carpet which she brought to Montreal, and then, when she separated from Bahram, he sent it to her in Toronto. Here she had to buy most of her furniture from the Salvation Army or garage sales.

When I first met Bahram, he asked me what I remembered about Afsaneh, about when she left him and came to Toronto, to our place. She arrived on a weekday afternoon. Tuesday or Wednesday, I don't remember. Afsaneh didn't look well, she looked pale and dishevelled. Ramin wasn't home, he was working late. I made tea and asked her if she had eaten. She said yes. I asked about her husband. She didn't answer directly. Then she apologized for being tired and said she hadn't slept last night. I offered her our only bedroom. At that time we lived in a one-bedroom apartment. Then I called Ramin and told him. He came home quickly.

"Where is she? he asked.

"She's sleeping."

"Where?"

"In the bedroom."

"Have you made something for dinner?"

"No."

Actually I hadn't thought about dinner. Whenever we had guests, Ramin cooked.

"Order a pizza," I said.

"You don't like pizza." he said.

"Afsaneh might like it."

Without answering, he went to the kitchen. He made rice with sauce and a salad. Waiting for Afsaneh to wake up, he lit a cigarette.

"You aren't supposed to smoke inside the house," I said.

He put out his cigarette, looking disturbed. I didn't like the way he looked at me.

Afsaneh woke up, washed her face, brushed her hair and came out to the living room. She still looked pale and vulnerable. Ramin went to her. Afsaneh threw herself in his arms and sobbed. Then she collected herself quickly and pulled away from him. Damon and I watched. Ramin invited her to sit down.

I served tea and cookies. There was a heavy silence. I guessed something had happened and waited for Afsaneh to speak. In a quiet voice she asked us, if it wasn't a problem, could she stay a few nights with us, while she looked for another place to live. Ramin and I said she could stay as long as she liked. I didn't want to have her in my home, but I couldn't refuse her. From the beginning of our acquaintance she hadn't been honest with me. I could see she didn't take me seriously, that she considered herself superior. Perhaps she regarded me as a child because I was younger.

Later, she told me I was more clever than I let on. What she said sometimes confused me, and when I asked her to explain, she was reluctant.

Yes, she was older than me. After she moved to Toronto, we saw each other more often. And then I could certainly say I was in a better position than she was. She had no money, no husband, no children. She had a job as a child care assistant in a daycare. And yet she showed a great deal of confidence, exactly the same Afsaneh as she had been in Iran, without any change or loss of self-esteem. And I've seen many Iranians metamorphose here —like Mahboobeh and Mehdi — and lose their dignity and self- confidence. Once I heard Mehdi tell Ramin, "I feel like a nobody here. I don't recognize myself. The Mehdi who once was, is dead. I don't even have the strength to face my own child."

"How can that be?" Ramin asked. "You're imagining things."

"I'm not imagining. That's what my wife and my children think of me, it's the reflection I see in their eyes. In Iran, I was somebody, with people working under my direction. My job was satisfying me intellectually and economically. Here, I'm nobody. I don't like my job, it's a chain around my neck. I do it because I have no choice."

But Afsaneh never changed. She used to say, "Human beings are human beings everywhere. It's not important what you do, it's important to give value to the work you do. When you degrade yourself, others degrade you, too."

Ramin, Mehdi and Mahboobeh admired her. Once we were at Mehdi's. I was in the kitchen, warming milk for Damon, and they were talking about Afsaneh. It was when Afsaneh was living in the shelter. Sometimes she came to visit us. I heard Ramin say, "To me, Afsaneh is like a tree — with many branches. A tree with strong roots, that won't shake in the wind. She provides shade to lay under and rest."

Mahboobeh answered, "There are few women like her."

I don't know what Mehdi said, but all of them laughed. I went to the living room, burning with anger. I screamed at Ramin for no reason. I wanted to tell him I was sorry he had lost his enveloping shade. But I controlled myself and apologized, saying I had a headache, and I didn't utter another word until we went home. I showed Ramin a new side of myself, and he learned not to talk about Afsaneh in front of me. This Afsaneh wasn't the same Afsaneh as in Iran, proud of her wealth, her education and her home. Here, she had nothing — no husband, child, or wealth. Nothing to boast about. I always wanted to know why she couldn't bear a child. Later, Bahram told me. Well, she married a crazy man. Yes, he really was mad. If he wasn't crazy he wouldn't have sterilized himself. But then if he hadn't done that, I wouldn't be talking about him. He certainly would have stayed with Afsaneh and had a few children by now. And I would be with Ramin.

Three or four days after Ramin disappeared, the telephone rang. I answered. I didn't feel well. I heard a man introduce himself as Bahram, say he was Afsaneh's ex-husband and he would like to see me. At first, I wasn't interested in talking to him. I had no love for Afsaneh, why would I be interested in seeing her husband? I excused myself, saying I wasn't feeling well. I really wasn't well. I was in the early stage of pregnancy and feeling sick all the time. I said I couldn't see anyone. Speaking formally and politely, he persisted. He said he wouldn't bother me for more than a few minutes. He called me Khanum. I said to myself, it wouldn't do any harm to see him. I was curious about him. What sort of man had Afsaneh chosen? I thought he might be special, different from other men. In the two years Afsaneh had lived in Toronto, she had suitors, but she showed no interest in marrying again or even having a boyfriend. The principal of her school asked her to marry him and she refused. Now I'm certain she loved Ramin. But I was blind and didn't notice it before.

Bahram came to express his condolences and tell me he was responsible for the "incident." I didn't understand; what did he mean? After two years of separation from Afsaneh, how was he responsible? Then it crossed my mind they might be having some on-going relationship, might be seeing each other without telling us about it. How do I know what people do?

It was one of those hot summer days, and there was no air conditioner in our place. A humid, hazy day and I didn't feel well. Damon was waking up from his afternoon nap, pestering me for his Baba. I thought he might have dreamt about his father. I was impatient and angry and didn't know what to do with him. When he saw Bahram, he was surprised and quieted. He stared at him. I was shocked, too. Bahram looked like Ramin. I don't know what happened to me. I started to cry, something I hadn't done since Ramin disappeared. I had been more angry than sad, cursing Afsaneh and Ramin constantly. I never thought they might have drowned, and because of that I didn't feel sorrow, just anger and hate. My tears were for my desperate situation, not for Ramin. Without a word Bahram hugged me. His action was soothing. As I sobbed, I wanted to put my head on his chest and keep him forever. He was tall. I didn't even reach his shoulders. Then I regained control, wiped my tears and apologized.

"I understand," he said, "it must be hard for you."

His way of talking and his manner were a great relief to me. He stared at me, as if he could see inside me what disturbed me, but I was attracted to him. I went to the kitchen to fetch him a drink of juice. He followed and offered the drink to me, pouring another one for Damon. The sympathy in his eyes, in his voice, as he offered help, was pleasing and surprising. I didn't know what to say. I couldn't utter a word of appreciation or thanks. He played with Damon, gaining his friendship and confidence. Saying good-bye, he told me he would stay in Toronto a few more days, and would like to get to know me better. It didn't cross my mind that he might want to support me and take care of me. I knew nothing about him.

Whenever I had asked Afsaneh to talk about Bahram, she refused. She wouldn't talk about living with Bahram. Her past was the time before she married. And usually, she talked with Ramin. They shared their memories. I always imagined they had secrets. When I was with them, they were quiet and talked of ordinary things. Afsaneh was a strange, taciturn woman. Bahram, too, was unusual. I mean he is unusual. Living with him isn't easy. That could be one reason Afsaneh left him.

I came to know him better later on, and discovered how complicated he was. I mean is. He's reluctant to get friendly with people, he keeps his distance even with me. He has no friends, especially no Iranian friends. He says Iranians aren't worth being friends with. He considers himself a cut above others. He might be right; he's educated, has a respectable job and an expensive house. In the beginning he didn't treat me badly. If Bahram hadn't shown up in my life, what would have happened to me? The day he called and said he wanted to see me, I asked myself: what for? What does he want from me? Who's Bahram anyway? I didn't feel like putting up with anybody. I had called my parents in Iran, to see if they could come to Toronto. I knew it was impossible. How can I invite them? Where was the money to come from? Only Mahboobeh and Mehdi, and sometimes Fataneh, came to see me or to take me visiting. Mahboobeh talked to me a lot. The kind of things people say in these kinds of situations. But talk solved nothing.

The day Bahram came to my place, I felt a window open in my life. His presence and manner were soothing and cheering. Then he asked me to dine with him in a restaurant. I didn't want to accept. I thought it wouldn't be proper to eat with a stranger in a restaurant less than a week after Ramin went missing. I wasn't that kind of person. Since I had married Ramin at sixteen, it had never crossed my mind to deceive him, though sometimes I tired of him and dreamed up an imaginary man for myself. Life with Ramin was sometimes boring. He was very serious about his duty, whatever it was. Stepping out of line never occurred to him. The principles he had learned in Iran, in his political groups, he insisted on here too, even though he knew life was different. Then when he found his honest effort didn't amount to anything, he became angry and thought something was wrong with him. I was angry that he didn't want to accept reality. Sometimes I wondered whether I should separate from him. I felt sorry for him, and I liked him in many ways. Although I wasn't in love with him, I was sort of committed to him since I was a child. My aunt had called me her daughter-in-law since I could remember. I was the only daughter of the two sisters. Ramin never dared cross me or disagree with me. I decided everything about our lives. He was obedient and very obliging, so much so he sometimes seemed like a fool. I could easily take advantage of him and use him as I liked. But Bahram is smart. I can't read his mind. He reads my mind very quickly. I can't play games with him or cheat him. He decides everything about our life and makes me follow him.

Even though I was impressed with Bahram and didn't want to end our first meeting, that first night I didn't go out to dinner with him. "What about tomorrow night?" he asked. I didn't know what to say.

"I'm going back to Montreal the day after tomorrow. I would like to know you, to have you tell me about your life and what you are going to do without Ramin. Perhaps I can find a way to help you. I know you will have a hard time, you are so young and you have a small child."

He didn't know I was pregnant with another baby. I accepted his invitation for the next day and didn't tell anyone about it. He took me to an expensive restaurant outside Toronto. I didn't know where we were going. Later on, when we often ate in that restaurant, I figured out it was in the suburb of Markham. I was wondering whether to wear make-up. I wanted to wear my green lenses and let my hair down over my shoulders. Yet, I felt guilty. I didn't talk to Mahboobeh about Bahram's visit or about going out to dinner. I told her he telephoned, but I didn't tell her he came to my place and invited me to a restaurant. Actually, I saw something in his eyes that I couldn't believe. Even though my sixth sense was working very well, I wasn't sure. In Iran, too, I acted quickly with the help of my sixth sense and didn't let Afsaneh take Ramin away from me. I didn't have any reason to talk to Mahboobeh about Bahram. Mahboobeh said, "Ramin will come back." To me, it was clear as daylight that Ramin, wherever he had gone with Afsaneh, whether he was dead or alive, wouldn't be back. I knew Ramin very well. He wasn't a person who would abandon his family. I was sure something terrible had happened to him but Mahboobeh kept saying, "He might come back, their bodies weren't found." I was sure something had happened to both of them. Why would they leave their tent and car in the campground and disappear?

I didn't want to talk about my relationship with Bahram to anybody because I wanted to know him better. The way he looked at me touched my heart. Talking about these things doesn't seem nice and proper, but whatever happened, my heart wasn't under my control. Bahram attracted me. He was strong and soft. He was the kind of man who is attractive to women. Maybe because of his money and his position. Later, when I complained to Fataneh that he didn't take me seriously, Fataneh said I'd been fooled by his air of manliness. She might be right. Bahram was a real man who seemed to have great power and made an impression on me. Ramin wasn't like him at all. For me, what Fataneh said wasn't important. She's a feminist and I don't agree with her about men. She doesn't make sense to me. I don't want to be a nun like her and not have relationships with men. I don't believe in equal rights. A woman is a woman, and a man is a man — two different genders. A woman should know how to take advantage of her man and not ignore her rights. But just talking won't do any good. A woman should follow her instinct. Fataneh knew I didn't let Ramin ignore me. Bahram, well, yes, many times he ignored me, especially recently. But I know what to do from now on. He should know, he had no right to humiliate me, or...

Better not to think about it yet. I have to make him understand I'm not the same Negar I was last week or last month. If he wants to stay with me, he has to change his behaviour. He has to be like he was last year, at the beginning of our relationship, when he took Damon and me to the restaurant that night. I enjoyed it very much. Damon was a quiet child, and didn't object or cry for anything. We ordered a hamburger for him which he liked very much. What a restaurant! I never imagined such a place. The waiters treated us as if I were Princess Diana. Bahram didn't take his eyes off me. He said he couldn't believe Ramin's wife was so young and beautiful. It was as if I was high in the clouds, dreaming. I thought, has he fallen in love with me? Later, he said he felt sympathy for me, I seemed very vulnerable. He wanted to help me. Actually, he was good to me for his own benefit, not out of love. He wanted to compensate for his sin. His sin? What sin? Even when he had told me everything, I didn't believe he had committed a sin. I had become dependent on him. His past, whatever it was, wasn't important to me. Everything he had done mattered to him, not to me. I told myself, if he really is guilty, he'd be in jail. I thought he was making a big deal about his "sin", as he called it. Support was more important to me, and he had decided to give it. He made a good life for me, a life I hadn't dreamed of. Whether his past was clean or not, he was good to me and to my children. If he had really murdered someone, he'd be in jail by now.

In the first weeks, he talked a lot about his past. He encouraged me to talk too. He wanted to get to know the real me.

He traveled to Toronto the following week as well. Thursday night to Sunday night, and every night he took Damon and me to a restaurant for dinner.

He came to my place a few times. I didn't say anything to Mahboobeh about it. I felt shy. I had fallen in love with Bahram; a strange love beyond my control. To tell the truth, I was ashamed of this love. He spent money lavishly on me. He brought me an expensive dress from Montreal. For Damon, he bought expensive toys we could never afford. Well, what could I do? Should I have sent him away and waited for Ramin, whom

I didn't believe would come back? Any woman in my situation would be enamoured of him. He talked to me, amused me, when we were together. When he tired of talking, he asked me to talk about Afsaneh and Ramin.

I didn't want to talk about them, but about memories from my childhood; about my father who was a bank employee, and my mother, a vice-principal in an elementary school. She took me to school with her when I was small. There were always women and girls around to love me. I had pale white skin and blond hair, unusual among Iranians, and everybody loved and spoiled me. I told him that life outside our country ripped the happiness out of my life. I had such a hard time here in Canada that if I lived for a hundred years, I would never forget it. I talked about life in Turkey, where I was depressed and wanted to go back to Iran. I cried night and day and made Ramin sick of me. I called my parents and told them I wanted to return. My mother cried on the phone, and begged me not to. I think Siamak had just been executed, and they were afraid if I returned, I would be arrested too. They sent us money. Later we found out they had sold their house to send us money. Ramin said that when we got to Canada, we'd work and send them money to buy another house. It didn't happen.

Life in Turkey was so terrible that sometimes I was tempted to throw myself out the hotel window. I wasn't ready for that kind of life. Ramin was twenty years old and my parents had put me in his care. They sent us into exile to protect me. When Siamak was arrested they panicked. I wasn't seriously involved in politics. Partly it was my fault. What I didn't tell Bahram was that I had wanted to leave Iran. At the time many young people went abroad. Girls and boys who had someone in another country, a brother or a sister. The universities were closed. Anyone with a high school diploma, who couldn't go to school in Iran, tried to leave Iran to continue their education. Many families emigrated and were uprooted. There were advertisements everywhere for family furniture sales. Boys were sent out mostly to avoid military service and being sent to the front line of the war with Iraq. Emigration and displacement were like diseases I caught.

Life in our home was unbearable after Siamak was arrested. My parents wouldn't let me go to school. Maman and Baba were in mourning, as if Siamak was already executed. Every day they went to Evin for news of him. At home, they were anxious about me, afraid our house might suddenly be surrounded by guards, we would all be arrested and sent to jail. It happened to many families. Ramin visited less, and whenever I called his house, he wasn't there. Imagining he might be with Afsaneh made me miserable. My mother wouldn't let me go out, even to my aunt's. She didn't like me to be alone with my cousins. There was no longer any talk about marrying Ramin. Ramin also kept his distance from me, especially once Afsaneh was in his life. His behaviour toward me changed. I realized I was going to lose everything. Our house was cold, and sad as a cemetery. My parents controlled me strictly. I told myself I had to do something. I lied. I said a close friend of mine had been arrested. My parents rushed me to Isfahan. A few days later Ramin came. We married. It took a few months for our parents to arrange a smuggler to take us out of the country. We crossed the mountains on horseback, walking every night. We spent the days in small villages among Kurds who were very kind and helpful, especially when they found out we were newly-weds. We arrived safely in Turkey, and I suffered more, even though no danger threatened me, no jail and execution, no Afsaneh.

Before leaving Iran, I suggested to Ramin that we go to see Afsaneh. I told him it wasn't fair to leave Afsaneh without saying goodbye. Ramin was reluctant. He wanted to go see her alone. But I insisted I would see her too. I was sure she wasn't a rival anymore and couldn't touch Ramin.

When I saw her place, I was jealous. Ramin had captured a good prey, but I didn't let him eat her. I wanted to show her she had under-estimated me, thinking of me as a child. The day we went mountain climbing, the way she looked at me hurt me deeply. It was degrading and I couldn't forget it. I showed her I could defend myself. For two hours at her home, I chatted and laughed happily. I sat close to Ramin, holding his hand in mine to show her who I was. Ten years later, how did I know she would show up again and pry him out of my hands? God knows what has happened to them. I don't believe they're alive. If they had gone to the moon, there would be news from them by now. But that day at Afsaneh's, I was the happiest woman in the world. Happier when I noticed Afsaneh was so disturbed. I had made her understand that she shouldn't undervalue me. She tried to appear glad about our marriage. She wished us good luck, long life together and a dozen children. I laughed and said, "A dozen? Who wants to take care of so many children?" "You should give birth to a dozen children," I added. She didn't answer. Her indifference didn't hurt me this time, because I knew why she was so upset. She went to the kitchen and stayed there a long time. After a while I followed her. I didn't let Ramin get up. I saw her standing by the window, gazing at the mountains. When she noticed me, she opened the fridge door and looked for something. Then I met her eyes. There were tears in them. She had cried and that pleased me. She sent me to the living room, saying she'd be there in a minute. When she came back, she was still upset. Ramin was quiet. That day I was the only person who spoke. I was happy and victorious. I was the winner. For a few days, Ramin was sulky and quiet. He was usually silent. Perhaps it was only when he was with me that he didn't like to talk. Years later, when Afsaneh appeared again and they saw each other more often, Ramin wasn't quiet. He talked to Afsaneh a lot.

At the beginning of my acquaintance with Bahram, he wanted me to talk about Afsaneh. I told him Afsaneh came to our place from Montreal, and then she found a place in a shelter and left. After that she became one of our friends. She was like a sister to Ramin and me. Damon loved her very much. She was so kind to us, I didn't have any reason to cut her out of our lives. Whenever she came to see us, she brought something for us, especially something for Damon. She was employed quickly. She knew French very well, had learned English and read a lot. Sometimes I envied her because she was independent, living on her own, and even in hard times, never asked for help. And she had her own ideas. When I said these things to Bahram, he asked, "Did she ever talk about me?"

I was too shy to tell him the truth. Whenever I asked her about Bahram, she made a face. Once, she told me Bahram didn't exist in her life and she tried to erase him from her memory.

I said, "No, Afsaneh didn't talk to me about her past."

And it was true, Afsaneh never talked to me about her past, except one night when we were camping. Majid was there too. Majid was a dentist, separated from his wife. He was looking for a wife. He liked Afsaneh and proposed to her several times, indirectly. Afsaneh didn't accept. On that camping trip, I didn't know what she said to him, but he left after a night. That night, Afsaneh was either drunk or something else had happened to her. She had taken some of us to the lake at night and we swam. Sitting around a camp fire there was a discussion about genies. Afsaneh talked about her childhood, about Ozra, her childhood maid who told her tales of genies. Afsaneh insisted that genies existed. Everybody laughed at her, but she held to her belief, saying that when she was a child, genies were her playmates.

Mehdi said, "I could believe everything about you, except that you would be superstitious."

"I'm not superstitious," Afsaneh said, "I believe in them."

"Still?" Mahboobeh asked.

"Yes," Afsaneh said.

Mahboobeh said, "Believe what? That genies exist? That they exist right here?"

"Yes, I do, yes, they exist," Afsaneh said seriously.

"Well, Miss Magician, show us some big genies," Mehdi said mockingly.

Afsaneh, upset by his ridicule, said, "When you don't want to believe, how can I prove it to you? Genies don't show themselves to everybody."

Ramin changed the subject, and I never dared ask her whether she really believed in genies. Ramin never talked to me about Afsaneh.

Bahram said Afsaneh had talked to him a lot about genies. On their honeymoon, they had gone to the Hotel Ramsar. Afsaneh liked to swim in the sea at night. She used to say at night she could see the genies and she danced with them in the darkness.

I believed Afsaneh was a little crazy. Or that sometimes she acted crazy. For example, her love for children. She couldn't bear Damon's crying. She cried with him. I told her once, "Suppose you had children, what would you do then

"Perhaps I wouldn't be so sensitive. I'd get used to their crying."

Like I had become used to the hardship of life in exile, to Siamak's death, to being far from my family. Sometimes I imagine Siamak didn't exist. Sometimes I forget I'm far from Maman and Baba. This last year, living with Bahram, the distance between life in Iran and here became wider. When I had just met Bahram, when I first went to live with him, I wanted to invite Maman and Baba to come here and see how I live. But Bahram didn't like the idea. He didn't refuse to send them an invitation, but every time I suggested it he ignored me. I wanted to marry him first and then invite Maman and Baba. But Bahram wouldn't marry me. He said, "What's the problem with our life as it is? Here many couples prefer to live together without getting married. Society has accepted this kind of arrangement. The government recognizes the same rights for them as for husbands and wives. What more do you want?"

I couldn't tell him my parents would be against it. I didn't have the guts to talk to him openly.

When he found out I was pregnant, he asked me to get an ultrasound, to find out if it was a boy or a girl. He said, "I'd like our baby to be a girl."

I wanted to laugh. "Our baby." As if he had planted it in my womb. We both knew he wasn't the real father. But I wanted him to consider himself my baby's father. After four months I had no hope of Ramin's return. Bahram couldn't have a child of his own. Well, now he would have two children. He was certainly very happy.

When he found out the baby was a girl, he was ecstatic. He bought me an expensive necklace. And a maternity dress at the Fairview Mall. We ate dinner in a restaurant and celebrated with champagne. He lifted his glass and said, "Cheers to Afsaneh."

Unbelievable, as if a horn was growing on my head. Afsaneh! Was Afsaneh alive?

He saw my surprise, smiled and said, "The little Afsaneh. The one who is not born yet."

To tell you the truth, his toast hurt me a lot. Why Afsaneh? Was there a shortage of names?

Annoyed, I told him, "My daughter's name is Negin. I always wanted to have a daughter and call her Negin, a name that's like mine."

"I told you," he warned me seriously, "her name will be Afsaneh."

So she was called Afsaneh even before her birth. I didn't have the nerve to call her Negin when she was born. Although, for a few weeks, I did call her Negin when Bahram wasn't home. Then it crossed my mind to call her Afi instead – short for Afsaneh, which he accepted. But from now on for me she is Negin, not Afsaneh or Afi.

That night I told myself, okay. Let it be Afsaneh, I'll concentrate on something else. I said, "I would like us to get married legally before my baby is born. I want my baby to have a legal father."

Mocking me, he said, "What's the difference between a legal and an illegal father? What good is Ramin, who is a legal father for Damon?"

His mood changed. I couldn't mention my parents' trip to Canada. Later on, when I talked about it, he promised to send an invitation, always a promise that never happened.

The day that baby girl was born, Bahram was beside me. He caressed me, held my hands in his, comforting me. When the baby was born, he took her in his arms, like the real father all the nurses in the delivery room imagined him to be.

When Bahram had first found out I was pregnant, he looked at me suspiciously and said, "Are you sure the baby is mine?"

It crossed my mind to tell him yes, but I hadn't forgotten that he told me he couldn't have a child. I explained, "I was already pregnant. Actually, Ramin left me, because of my pregnancy."

He said, "Why didn't you tell me before?"

I didn't know what to say. I started to cry.

"Why are you crying?" he asked, surprised.

"What's wrong with having a sister or a brother for Damon?"

"But you told me Ramin left because he was in love with Afsaneh."

"Yes, but he made my pregnancy an excuse to leave me. Ramin didn't like having children. Perhaps he thought children would tie him to his family, force him to stay with me. He said we didn't have a stable life here, we're not settled, we didn't have the right to bring another human being into this world. He forgot about me, that I am a woman. Ramin couldn't understand that. I wanted to have children. My mother wrote to me, why don't you want to have children? She certainly expected me to bear her grandchildren. Well, she had a right. Siamak died too young. If I didn't have children, our family would come to an end with my generation. Ramin insisted on not having children, but I stopped taking birth control pills without saying a word to him."

When I spoke about my life to Bahram, he looked at me,

surprised, and listened. When I became quiet, he said, "You're not the idiot I thought you were at our first meeting. You're a clever woman."

"What do you mean?" I asked.

"You know how to get your way." Then he warned me, "You shouldn't play games with me. I won't stand for it." His tone was alarming.

When he found out about my pregnancy, Bahram came to Toronto; he told me he wanted to sell his apartment in Montreal and move to Toronto to live with me. He treated me as if I was fragile, as if there was a risk I would fall apart at any moment. That week he took Damon and me to Montreal to stay for a few days. His life was so lavish I thought Afsaneh was crazy to leave him.

Until that time I hadn't spoken to anybody about my relationship with Bahram. I didn't dare talk to Mahboobeh. What would she think of me? I told her he sometimes called, asking how I was or if I needed anything. When he decided to move to Toronto, I couldn't hide it anymore, and told Mahboobeh. She had come to visit me. She saw Damon's expensive toys and noticed I was not as upset or disturbed as I was when Ramin first disappeared. Damon told her Baba Bahram had bought those toys for him. Mahboobeh looked at me strangely, asking, "Is he right?"

"Yes, he's right. Bahram is very kind to Damon and me." I said, "he's going to move to Toronto to live."

"In the same place with you?"

"Yes, well, maybe."

"And have you agreed?"

"Shouldn't I? Should I wait for Ramin until he is fed up with Afsaneh and comes back again? I'm not sure he will. Was it my fault Ramin betrayed me, with a baby in my belly and a four-year-old child, to follow his old love?"

"But if he returns?" she said.

"He won't. Afsaneh has either whisked Ramin away and won't

let him return to us. Or she's trapped him with her genies. It's already two months since they disappeared, with no news. Do you think Ramin is such an irresponsible man that he would leave us, without any contact, even Damon? He loved Damon more than his own life."

Mahboobeh looked at me surprised, in a way she hadn't before.

"What do you suggest I do?" I said, "Send Bahram away? He has accepted my child and me and is generous and kind, what should I do? Do nothing and wait for Ramin to return? What if Ramin never returns. If Ramin loved me, he wouldn't have gone off with Afsaneh. A man like Bahram doesn't come along often."

"I've heard Afsaneh's ex-husband is wealthy. He has his Ph.d. in computer science and a good job. He's not forced to survive delivering pizzas like poor Ramin. Well, what do you want then?"

"Mahboobeh," I said, "I didn't expect you to judge me like this. Do you think I wrote Bahram a love letter, or that I knew him before? You know very well that Afsaneh never talked to anybody about Bahram. You know what kind of person Afsaneh is."

"Afsaneh wasn't a bad person," she said, "she didn't do anything to you."

"Didn't she?"

"You don't know what has happened."

"I know. I told you before, the day Ramin left home, he was angry about my pregnancy. He left home, as he did many times when he was angry and didn't want to say something hurtful to me, or behave badly. In less than an hour Afsaneh showed up. She rarely came to visit us without telling us. But that day she appeared suddenly. It was during the week. I told her everything. I told her because I have nothing to hide. How did I know Afsaneh was waiting for such a thing to happen so she could grab Ramin? Believe me, I noticed joy in her eyes. She caressed me and Damon. She was disturbed, but she kissed me, hugged me, and left saying goodbye as if she knew she was leaving forever. She had probably made her decision at that moment. Yes, she left us for good. Then her tent and car were found by the lake."

Mahboobeh listened to me in silence, as if she didn't know me, or had met me for the first time. She said, "Negar, I know nothing about Ramin and Afsaneh's relationship or about you and Bahram. I know what you've told me. I didn't know that Afsaneh loved Ramin years ago. I just observed she was a close friend of yours. Ramin didn't appear to do anything wrong. If he did, you'd know. You can't deny that."

"I don't deny it," I said, "it might seem that Ramin spent all his time with us. But I couldn't control his mind. His relationship with me was mostly a duty. He always used to say, your parents entrusted you to me. Sometimes I felt he slept with me out of duty."

"Why haven't you ever complained about him? You used to talk all the time about your life. Why didn't you say that Ramin didn't love you?"

"What kind of talk is this Mahboobeh? What woman wants to say her husband doesn't love her? Then you might have told me, why stay with him? Leave him."

"You might be right," she said, "perhaps I didn't know Ramin very well. Mehdi always admired him. He used to say, he is a simple direct guy. Well, he was, wasn't he?"

"Yes, he was. But his heart wasn't with me. He never forgot Afsaneh's love. I don't know, perhaps we shouldn't have married. That was my fault. Yes, I confess, it was my fault. But well, it happened. The situation forced us to marry. And then we had a child. He shouldn't have left me for another woman. I could have done the same to him. As many women do. I'm pretty and young. If I wanted I could have chosen another man, but I didn't, because I loved my family. I didn't want Damon to suffer from our separation. I didn't want my parents in Iran to worry about me. They have suffered more than enough. I didn't want to make it worse.

You can't imagine why I'm with Bahram. I wish you could see how he treats me, admires me, how he takes care of me. You can't believe it, because you haven't seen it with your own eyes."

The day I was talking to Mahboobeh I was pretty sure of myself and Bahram's love for me. I wasn't boasting. Bahram appreciated my beauty, especially when I wore my green lenses with my blond hair.

He used to say, "It suits you very well. You look European. If you didn't speak, nobody would recognize you as an Iranian."

He never scolded me for spending time in front of a mirror. He wasn't like Afsaneh and Ramin, embarrassing me because I wasn't a bookworm like them. He told me, "Your time is yours, you spend it as you like and enjoy yourself."

When Mahboobeh left, I realized I shouldn't call her any more. There was a gulf between us. After Bahram bought a house in Richmond Hill and we began to live together, my relationship with Mahboobeh was pretty much over. Bahram didn't like Mahboobeh and Mehdi, and told me to forget about my past and my Iranian friends. The only part of the past he wanted to keep was Afsaneh. He wanted to talk to me about her. It was hard for me to talk about her. I hated her the first time I saw her. I have a right to hate her. She was better than me at everything. She was very articulate, had a vast knowledge of life. She was university educated, in France and Iran. When I met her, she was in her last year of psychology at the University of Tehran. Although she didn't have a very pretty face, she wasn't ugly either. As Mahboobeh used to say, the way one behaves is more important than the way one looks. Some people have a face like a monkey and can still look beautiful. Afsaneh was one of them. She's a snake charmer, attractive and able to be friends with everyone even though she's not beautiful. Everyone who met her was enchanted by her. But I hated her. When she entered my life the second time, I still didn't like her. But she was so kind to us that I yielded. I couldn't avoid being grateful for her love. Especially her love for Damon. My child desperately needed that love. He had no relatives here, no sisters, no brothers, no aunts, no uncles, or cousins. Afsaneh took their place and nourished Damon with her love. Whenever I wanted to go somewhere, Afsaneh lovingly volunteered to take care of Damon. I was sure she would be careful. I knew she would take care of him, even better than me.

When I first knew Afsaneh and was worried she would take Ramin from me, I thought of arranging for her to meet Siamak. In those days, anyone who was politically active or didn't share the government's ideology lived at risk of persecution and arrest. Siamak was in danger. At my suggestion Siamak went to Afsaneh's place to hide from the revolutionary guards who were looking for him. I imagined Afsaneh and Siamak would get to know each other, and something might happen between them. After a few days, Siamak left Afsaneh's. I don't know what happened. A few days later, Siamak was arrested in the street. Ramin didn't tell me why Siamak left Afsaneh's. I poured out my anger on Afsaneh, cursing her openly in front of Ramin. I believed that if Afsaneh hadn't kicked Siamak out of her house, he wouldn't have been arrested. I couldn't understand why she didn't let him stay a few more days.

When I told this story to Bahram, he said, "I can't believe you could be so shrewd."

"It wasn't shrewdness. I didn't want anything bad to happen to either of them. Siamak was popular with girls. At university, we always had phone calls from girls who wanted to be friends with Siamak."

At the beginning of my friendship with Bahram, especially, he talked about his past, his childhood, and how when he was a newcomer in Canada, he dated an African girl, an Arab, I think, who became pregnant.

"I wanted to marry her," he said, "her skin colour didn't matter to me. I loved her. She was very kind to me. My father stopped me from marrying her."

Her name was Hanna. I wished my daughter was called Hanna, too. Hanna is a beautiful name, much nicer than Afsaneh. At least I didn't hate the name, because I never met Hanna.

He talked about Behnaz, his sister, a year younger than himself.

"She drowned in the Caspian Sea," he said, "it was my fault. If I had warned her a moment earlier that a big wave was getting close to the shore, she would have run to the shore and the wave wouldn't have pulled her into the sea. I didn't and it happened. I have never been able to forget it and forgive myself."

I soothed him, "You were a child too. Perhaps you couldn't speak – your tongue was tied."

"No, it wasn't that," he said, "I hated her. She was competing with me. She was smarter than me. Her marks were better. Everything that was given to me, was given to her too. My mother showed more love for me than her. I was born after three girls. Later on I realized my mother got pregnant again in the hope of having another boy. After Behnaz's birth, my parents slept in separate bedrooms."

Once Bahram talked about his faults, I felt I could talk about my life. Well, nobody had committed suicide because of me or drowned in the sea. But I didn't marry Ramin out of love. It was to get out of Iran. My parents would never permit a girl of sixteen to leave on her own for Turkey or any other country. And if I had been too slow to act, Ramin would have slipped out of my hands. I talked to Bahram about these things. Later, he used them against me, said he had made a mistake about me, that I was playing a role. Once when I was angry with him, I mentioned Hanna. I said whatever I did, I had never caused someone to commit suicide. He slapped my face so hard I was dizzy. I picked up the phone to call the police. He took the phone from me and apologized, he was suddenly so nice to me that I forgot about it. After that I never dared talk rudely to him or say bad things about Afsaneh or Hanna. I was always cautious about what I was saying. Finally, I became cowed. In the beginning, he made me feel submissive through his kindness, generosity, and lavish spending, later he did it through physical power and authority. If I left, where would I find another man like him? No, in the last year, it never crossed my mind to leave him. I loved him, I was enthralled by him. I was scared of him, especially when he was drunk; he cursed me and couldn't stand Damon. But he never laid a hand on me again. He was probably afraid I'd call the police. Whenever he saw the police, he cursed them in a way that was unbefitting his polite, educated manner.

Last night I was so scared I decided to go to the police and tell them all about him. But then, when I remembered how much Bahram hated the police, I changed my mind. I decided to go to Mahboobeh's place instead. Then I changed my mind and thought I'd better go home. Arriving home, I was dead tired. I have to be careful. Now that I think it over, it seems I must have been imagining things. Bahram didn't want to hurt us. What reason would he have for drowning the three of us? I'm not his legal wife and the children aren't his either. He can leave us and go his own way. He's not crazy. Is he? Perhaps he is. Last night he was crazy.

He said, "Right now, Afsaneh and Ramin are at the bottom of the lake, making love. The genies have made a big palace for them and they're happy together. We'd better go visit them."

I'm sure he was drunk, unaware of what he was saying. But I was scared. I pretended to be sick. When he insisted on going sailing, I made excuses. I was cold, I had my period and cramps. I hated sailing. He had rented a boat. Most days we were on the lake, sailing. But I couldn't stand sailing at night. I was scared to death, with only the black lake below and the moon overhead. As they say: "When the moon is full, the witches appear and hurt people."

I can't live with him anymore. He has no right to set foot here. I'll show him a Negar he's never seen before. I can't live in horror and fear, with my son abused by his indifference and his screaming, while he lives as he likes, drinking and misbehaving. Perhaps Afsaneh bewitched him. She talked about genies to Damon. It made me angry. I told her, "You have no right to fill my child's head with superstition. It's the space and computer age and you amuse my child with genies!"

She said seriously, "Leave space and computers to those who invented them. I'm happier with my genies."

"If you want to be happy with genies, it's up to you," I said, "but I don't want my child raised with superstition."

Sometimes I think Afsaneh was abnormal, too. She might really have known some genies and fairies. Perhaps she had a way with words. Perhaps she bewitched people by talking. She probably bewitched Bahram. And Ramin, who went with her and didn't look back. Yes, she captivated Bahram. He said Afsaneh would never leave him alone. Sometimes I don't know whether he means my Afi, or his damned Afsaneh who ruined his life. He enlarged Afsaneh's photo and put it in the library. When I saw it for the first time, I was so hurt. I took it off the wall, and put it in the closet. He screamed at me, saying I couldn't even tolerate a photo. I had to yield, but to myself, I said, you are happy with only her photo. If she loved you, she wouldn't leave you.

I have to get rid of him. He's not easy to live with. He's not stable. Sometimes he's nice and spends money lavishly, saying nice things, and sometimes I can't bear him for even a minute. He's impatient and cross — screaming at Damon and me for no reason. He locks himself in the library, drinking. My children and I don't dare make noise. Sometimes he plays with Afsaneh for half an hour, but when he takes her into the library and closes the door, I'm scared. Awful thoughts cross my mind. I find an excuse to get the baby from him. If it isn't late, I go out. I put the children in the car and go to the mall or take Damon to the community center to play and fall asleep. I don't want Damon to make noise at home and make Bahram angry and violent. When I come home, Bahram is usually still in the library. I put the children to bed and watch TV with an earphone. I go to bed alone. He's not interested in sleeping with me anymore. Although being ignored hurts, I'd rather be left alone than insulted and then taken to a restaurant or given some new clothes.

These last few weeks, when he decided to go camping, Bahram was nice to me again and began asking for my opinion.

"Why should we go to the same spot where those two were last year?"

"What's the problem? In their memory, on the anniversary."

We dined in restaurants most nights. Bahram bought summer dresses and swimming suits for me, toys and clothes for Damon and Afi. He rented a cabin and a boat, talking all the time about camping, sailing on the lake, fishing, hiking, barbecuing, and so on. Damon was excited and asked questions all the time. But I was worried. I didn't want to go to that same spot. I said I didn't like camping. Even when we went with Ramin and Afsaneh and other friends, I didn't like it. Group camping was better, and we had a good time, but still I didn't enjoy it. One time Fataneh and Majid were with us, before Afsaneh showed up. Majid liked Fataneh, but when she talked about women's rights and feminism, he lost interest in her. He said life would be hard with that kind of girl. A year later Majid met Afsaneh and liked her very much. Afsaneh refused to even be friends with him. When we went camping, there was always political or feminist talk among the group. I never participated, sometimes I didn't even listen. Afsaneh was always passionate, like Fataneh, but I ridiculed their talk.

I suggested to Bahram that he ask Mahboobeh and Mehdi to come camping with us. Bahram made a face. They were Ramin's friends, he wanted nothing to do with them. I wondered, who are your friends then? He used to say Iranians aren't worth being friends with. I was angry with him. Wasn't he Iranian? As I am, and Afsaneh as well. But I couldn't argue with him. Sometimes I felt a lump in my throat, tears in my eyes, and turned from him.

Then he softened, saying, "what's the use of a friend? With so much to do, still you want someone to chat with and waste your time?"

I wished I could swear at him and be rid of him, but I was scared. I was afraid if I cursed him, he'd be rude and do what he wanted anyway.

I didn't realize why his behavior had changed. It didn't change overnight. Sometimes, very rarely, he was nice, gentle. Most of the time he was unbearable. Once he told me that living with me was a mistake. It hurt, but the next day he was gentle Bahram again.

To tell the truth, I don't know what to do with him. I'm scared of him. I love him and I hate him as well. If last night he hadn't insisted on sailing, we would probably be together now, and today we'd all be back home. How could I know what was in his head? His ramblings worried me. I could see something terrible in his eyes. There was no reason to take me and two small children sailing at night. We'd spent the whole day on the lake. Why at night, again? And exactly one year after Ramin and Afsaneh disappeared. He had made an awful decision about us. He was fed up with life, and wanted us to perish along with him. He was probably thinking I might commit suicide, like Hanna did. But I'm a different person. There's no reason I would do that. I'm not crazy like her. I have two children to raise. I'm not going to have a love affair like Ramin. My loves are my children. I loved Bahram because of my children. He must know that. Perhaps Afsaneh's premonition was going to come true. I shouldn't have told Bahram that story. It came to mind suddenly. He listened, unbelieving and said, "Did you make that up?"

"Why would I make it up? Afsaneh was superstitious. Wasn't her belief in genies a superstition? This Nowruz, when her seeds were rotten and she had to throw them away, she said, 'I'm afraid something bad will happen to us.' She called her uncle in France more often and even called Tehran to check on Ozra's grandchildren. They were the only people she had in Iran. She was always worrying that they might have a bad accident. She told us over and over that she was sure something bad might happen."

Bahram listened to me. Whether he believed me or not, I don't know. He was quiet for a while, which scared me. I shouldn't have talked to him. If Bahram had dangerous ideas about us, he might think they were pre-determined. No, it's not true. It's just my imagination. How can I find out if he really had decided to drown us in the lake? I have to wait and see what will happen.

Afi is crying. No not Afi, Negin. From now on, Negin. Bahram has to call her Negin. She's my child. Bahram is not her father, not any more. She's awake. I have to get up and nurse her, change her diaper. I have to continue with my life. He has probably made his decision by now. Dead or alive, it's the same to me. I have to take care of the children. Oh, Damon is awake too. I have to get up. I didn't sleep at all. What a terrible night. But it's over. I have to be hopeful. Whatever happens, I have to raise my children. They are my parent's grandchildren and will carry the family name.

❦ TWO ❦

❧ I want to sleep and not to live ☙
and in a sleep as sweet as death to dream.

Charles Baudelaire

"I KNEW SOMETHING would happen. I can't remember a time when my seeds failed to sprout. Not when Ozra was still alive and grew wheat and lentil for Nowruz, not even in France, during those cold springs, never. Here, too, last year, the sprouts were fresh and abundant. But this year, the seeds were rotten and I had to throw them away. I was sure something awful was going to happen."

Afsaneh sat on a picnic bench, leaning on the table, wearing gray shorts, running shoes and pale green socks. Her arms were bare, her hands rested on bare legs. Her hands and feet were numb, her heart heavy. She felt cold, not only on her skin, but in the blood chilling her veins. Her big black eyes sparkled with the glow following days of rapture. She pictured her last image of Ramin — old jeans, a checkered shirt, worn, dark blue running shoes, his shoulders bent, black hair touched here and there with gray, his face pale, and a determined look deep in his eyes. This image never left her mind.

"I knew you would leave me. From the first moment you came into my place, overcome with distress, I remembered the seeds and worried about an accident. But I didn't think it would happen to me. And now you're leaving. Do you remember? I told you."

"You must accept that my leaving has nothing to do with your seeds. Don't insist I stay, I have to go."

Afsaneh didn't insist. All night and all day, lying in the suffocationg air in the tent, sitting on this bench, under these trees, birds singing and mosquitoes stinging, they sat and talked. Finally he said, "I have to go. There are no second chances. If I make a mistake, I'll end up on the wrong path."

"You've already taken the wrong path. You have to have the guts to realize it. Acknowledge you've taken the wrong path."

"That's true. But I felt I had to."

"Now you don't have to."

"You don't understand and you don't have to understand. The lives of two or three others..."

"You've decided to sacrifice yourself. Siamak was martyred and you weren't. Now you want become a martyr too. That's it."

He turned away.

"He left me. I knew he would. He had to go. He wanted to go. To be a martyr. Sacrifice is part of his nature. Sacrificing! His family heritage. Their Siamak was martyred, became a hero. And Ramin has to measure up to Siamak. Sacrifice himself, to prove his identity."

A mosquito stung Afsaneh's arm. Her hand moved automatically to scratch. She came back to herself. A bird was singing sporadically. She listened to the bird's sad song. A breeze blew among the leaves, making them whisper.

"I wish I was part of nature, unfeeling and unable to think. Like this tree, just standing in place. To not know the pain of love and desire. I'd die every fall and bloom again every spring, I'd embrace the breezes and thunderstorms."

In front of her among tall, wide trees stood a young sapling with clear green leaves. Like a young man, wanting to claim his presence among the elders. Its leaves shook happily, as if a secret joy caressed it. Afsaneh was captivated by the tree. She didn't notice when the bird stopped singing and silence again surrounded her.

"I wish I was that tree. How beautiful and proud. And why not? It's not a slave of love like I am."

Afsaneh imagined Ramin lost on a dirt road, hidden behind a row of trees. Gone, like a sigh leaving her chest. Nights and days she had spent with him among these trees, inside that tent made for one person. Their story ended suddenly, leaving her obsessed with joy and sadness. The joy of being with Ramin, at one with his body and soul, a joy she dreamed of for many years. And then the sadness of his absence. Over like a story, a sweet story with a sharp ending. She wanted him back again.

"No, it won't happen. I know it won't. Insisting was useless. He's bound to his responsibilities, to his wife and children."

"What are you going to do tonight?"
She stayed mute, staring.

Afsaneh had been looking for a book about Hallaj in one of the bookstores on Revolution Street, close to the University of Tehran, and couldn't find it. A hand, young and skinny with black hair growing on it, stretched up to the same shelf and pulled out the book. She turned and looked at the man. Two black eyes in pale bony cheeks stared at her, amazed. A current of electricity sang through her body. She flushed. Then she regained herself and said, smiling, "I was looking for the same book."

The young man offered the book to her.

Afsaneh heard the bookseller's voice behind her back.

"Which book is it?"

The young man showed it to him.

"I'm sorry," the bookseller said, "it's the only copy we have."

The young man offered Afsaneh the book again. "I'm serious, you can have it."

"No, it's yours."

The young man put the book on the counter, searching his pockets. After a minute he pulled his hands out of his pocket. "I'm sorry, I don't have enough money," he said.

Afsaneh looked at the young man, smiling. Again, she noticed the spark in his eyes, and the blood rushed in her veins. She paid for the book, and left the bookstore along with the young man. Outside, on Revolution Street, sat tables filled with books.

"Would you like have a look at these?" she said. "We might find it here."

"No, I'd prefer to borrow it from you, after you read it."

"That's not a bad idea, then we could discuss it," she answered, feeling elation.

They walked east, in the early spring afternoon. A gentle breeze lessened the density of the air pollution. Hundreds of vehicles, including the Vahid Company two-story buses howled and roared by, leaving no room for chatting. They reached the Valiasr intersection. Evening crept on the afternoon. Car headlights came on. The air was heavier, vehicles were everywhere, blocking intersections. They stopped in front of a café. Afsaneh was thirsty and wanted to invite the young man to have an ice cream and cold drink with her. Then she remembered he said he had no money.

The man stretched out his hand, saying, "My name is Ramin. I should have introduced myself earlier."

Afsaneh smiled and said, "Afsaneh."

"It seems we should say goodbye to each other."

Does he know me from before? She thought. He looks friendly.

"Have I seen you before?" she asked.

"Maybe. I'm studying literature."

"I'm studying psychology. Just one term left before I'm finished."

"Perhaps I've seen you there, or in the demonstrations, or..."

"I haven't been at the demonstrations often and, even then, only as a spectator."

The young man's eyes were fixed on her. A current of hot and rapid blood started from her feet and ran to her chest and became a hot red flush on her cheeks. Her eyes, fixed on his, wouldn't move. Afsaneh regained herself abruptly, stretched her hand out, saying, "Goodbye" and walked to Revolution Square.

"Are you going back?"

She stopped, "My car is parked close to the bookstore."

Ramin walked toward her. "My house is near that area too."

The both laughed and there was a secret hidden in their laughter which they talked about a long time later. Walking, they talked ceaselessly, about everything. They started a topic and without finishing, started another one, until they stopped beside Afsaneh's green Renault.

"I remember you. I've seen you. I mean, I've seen your Renault. It's a unusual shade of green."

Afsaneh stared at him. There was something both familiar and strange about him, something that made her want to linger.

"What about an ice-cream?" she said, and then remembered he said he had no money. "Don't worry about the money, be my guest."

Ramin put a hand into his pocket and brought out bills.

"So, it was a trick?"

"There's always a way to make a friend."

A squirrel appeared among the trees and walked hurriedly to Afsaneh looking at her with small, black eyes. It probably expected something to eat. Afsaneh stared. The bird's song brought her back to herself again. A strange song, as if it had something to say to her but she didn't understand. A mosquito whizzed overhead and stung her cheek before she could flick it away.

"You sacrifice yourself for nothing. If Negar valued it, if

she appreciated your sense of duty, that would be different, but she…I can't understand how a person can devote himself to someone who doesn't value him. Why don't you want to understand? Why?"

"You can't feel what I feel. Negar is my problem, not yours. You know everything. Why should I explain? I promised her parents, I promised myself, Siamak, too. I have a duty."

"Duty, duty. You're always thinking of duty. She's an adult and a mature person. And you're devoting yourself for nothing. There are plenty of people like her in this world and you're…"

"Enough," he screamed, "enough preaching. I'm sure if you were in my place, you would do the same."

"No, I wouldn't," she screamed louder, "Bahram needed me too. He was a desperate person who suffered, too. He needed someone to console him. I couldn't. Why should I devote myself to him? It wasn't my fault he caused a young girl to commit suicide. It wasn't my fault he gave his child to a stranger and then sterilized himself. Why should I suffer because of his ignorance? You only live once."

"Your problem is different than mine. As you said, you didn't have any responsibility for his mistakes, but me…"

"You weren't responsible for Negar's life. You were just her cousin, not her father, or her mother."

"You know her parents entrusted her to me. And I promised them."

"Negar is not a child. She's a mature and wise woman. I'm sure she can handle her life. But you and her parents, and that Siamak who has become a saint for all of you, raised her like a doll, powerless. She takes advantage of this situation. Anyone in her place would do the same."

"I wish I could think as you do. I wish I could. But believe me, I can't. These last few nights, I tried hard. But I can't. Afsaneh believe me, I wouldn't be happy with you either."

"You don't want to be happy. Some people are born to be miserable. Misery is injected into them, it's in their blood. You're one of them. In you, love dies instead of blooming."

"You don't know me either. You can't understand what kind of misery I live. You can't and you don't want to."

"Perhaps you still think I'm a carefree landowner's daughter, who thinks only about love and enjoying my life."

"No, I never thought about you like that. You know very well I didn't."

"Perhaps you never loved me."

"What are you saying? Since I saw you in that bookstore, since that day, there hasn't been one single day that…"

"And now that we have each other, now that we're through the years of separation…"

"No, we aren't. Let it end right here."

"And you'll go back?"

"I have to. I can't leave Damon, or Negar with a baby in her…"

Afsaneh said nothing. A mosquito stung her neck, she felt the pain sharply. She didn't touch her neck. She saw Ramin putting on his shoes, tying his shoelaces. He stood in front of her.

"What are you going to do?"

She didn't answer.

"You'd better collect the stuff and go back to the city."

"The city? Which city?"

"Toronto."

"I won't go to Toronto. I'll go somewhere else to live."

"When?"

"I don't know. I might stay here tonight."

"Alone?"

"What's the problem?"

"Aren't you afraid?"

"Go and don't worry about me. I'm not afraid of anything. Not of night, or darkness, the lake, the forest or loneliness."

"I know. You won't be alone. The genies won't let you be alone."

He smiled, kissed her cheek and went away. And she remained motionless.

The afternoon was slowly losing light. A cold breeze, like an imprecise clock, reminded her of the coming night. Afsaneh was still sitting on the bench, staring into nothingness. She heard a conversation. The words didn't seem familiar to her, and she couldn't decide what language it was. A baby cried and then a woman called out a name, Sonia or Sofia, she couldn't quite hear it. Afsaneh was stuck to the bench. The sky was a soothing color. The trees put the day behind them and became amazingly still. Afsaneh was wrapped in the forest which had been there for thousands of years. The yearning to be one with nature was in her like a yearning for death.

"You wanted to be a poet. Do you remember this poem?
I hung my sadness for you
Framed by my heart,
On the walls of all my moments
And your memory
Like an altar for my prayer."

"That's not poetry. Life here allows me no time to write poetry."

"You don't give yourself time. You've even forgotten your dreams and desires."

"We all had desires. We all wanted to do something. Those who lost their lives had dreams too. At least they were honest with themselves and put their dreams ahead of their lives."

"And you feel guilty you aren't one of them. You always feel guilty, and don't want to accept the fact that their dreams were an illusion, a real mirage."

"Whatever their dreams were, they stayed true to their beliefs. They kept us aware of the meaning of humanity."

"Oh, stop it. All of you admire death, while it's life that's valuable. Look, look at this piece of land! These trees, this sky, the lake, look how magnificent they are! You've forgotten all about these wonderful things and admire only death, nothingness, darkness. You worship them. You're a stranger to life, a stranger to nature, to leaves, to breezes, to the seas. You don't have eyes and can't see the beauty. If you could look at a leaf on a tree, you would see a world of wonder in it. Nature doesn't care about human values. And because of that, nature is amazing. It's beautiful, it's soothing, it's accepting. If human beings stayed one with nature, your way of thinking would disappear and we'd all be happier."

"Afsaneh, all of this is just poetry. You can't condemn people who sacrificed their lives for their ideals."

"I'm not talking about your martyrs. You know very well I respect them. Have you ever heard me say anything against your Siamak, or the others? Yes, perhaps if I was in their place, I would do the same. I might prefer, as you say, to be a martyr rather than to confess and repent. But it didn't happen to me. It didn't happen to you, either. I'm sure if you had been arrested, you would now be lying beside Siamak, one more martyr to our history. But you chose to risk your life by fleeing. You saved yourself in order to live. I admired you, and now you regret it. This makes me angry. You came here to live, but you don't live. You're dying, little by little. Do you understand what I'm saying? You're dying. You won't be a martyr, but you'll die. You won't be considered a martyr. You are a person who left and has no place here. I condemn those who are alive and think only of death. People like you: a lover of life, of poetry, who forces himself to sacrifice for nothing. You deserve to live, not to die."

"What about my commitments?"

"Oh, stop it. Go and be happy with your commitments. Live with hate and name it commitment, responsibility, duty. Pretty words. Empty words."

And he went. The sunlight caressed the highest branches of
the trees. His departure left a cold shadow around her. The brick-
coloured tent was like a patch of fire in the surrounding. It gave a
sense of wonder to the area. Afsaneh heard footsteps coming
close.

"He came back, I knew he would."

A man passed on the dirt path, looked at her, and nodded
hello.

They were in a restaurant on Shemiran road. They'd finished
their ice cream. Afsaneh was waiting for Ramin to leave. But Ramin
didn't move.

"How about a piece of cake?" Afsaneh said.

"I'll pay this time."

"Okay, as long as it's not because you're a man."

"Not when I'm with you."

"Don't be so formal."

Outside the restaurant in Pahlavi Street renamed Valiasr after
the revolution, tall plane trees were illuminated by street lamps. A
few stores were still open, a pleasant light shone from their windows. Cars passed rapidly downhill. They finished their cake and
tea, and still they stayed.

"Don't you want to go home?" Ramin asked, "your mother,
and your father, won't they be worried about you?"

"No. There is nobody."

"You live alone?"

She nodded, "Yes."

Suddenly the electricity went off. The restaurant went dark.
Afsaneh and Ramin imagined an air attack and waited for a siren.
The street was lit by the occasional passing car. A gas lamp close
to the cash register was lit. It's wheezing noise filled the whole
restaurant. The waiter came and lit a candle on their table. Ramin
looked at his watch. "I have to go, or my mother will worry about
me."

They left the restaurant. Afsaneh's Renault was parked about thirty feet further on. They walked in silence, and both got into the car.

"To Revolution Street?" Afsaneh asked.

"No, I live around Seventeenth Shahrivar Square. But you can drive to your house, I'll get out along the way."

"You mean you live in Jaleh Square?"

"Yes, in the area of Abesardar."

"You told me you live near Revolution Square."

"A little lie."

A wave of joy passed through Afsaneh but no words slipped out. Quietly, she turned and looked at his profile in the passing light of the cars. There was a pale smile on his lips. She passed the Valiasr intersection. The streets were lit in this area, but neither of them noticed the electricity was on. Both were busy in their minds. They didn't speak.

"If you stop here, I'll get out."

"If you tell me your address, I'll choose the best route to your home."

The afternoon spread out like a heavy, middle-aged woman. Nature was a kind mother embracing her in its unusual silence. It was as if the trees shared her memories. Afsaneh had a genuine empathy for trees, land, sky, and wind. They embraced her, offered her comfort and sympathy. At that moment, if a close friend had been with her, Afsaneh wouldn't have spoken about what was happening to her. But surrounded by nature, the words flowed inside her and she imagined she was talking to trees, to the land and the lake. They listened in silence, and asked, "What are you going to do?"

They were in the Darakeh Mountains, sitting on a large rock. The narrow path curved among rocks to the summit. It was afternoon and the number of people going uphill was decreasing. Those returning walked downhill quickly. The middle-aged and families with small children arrived later and walked uphill with short, slow steps, stopping on their way to rest. It was their first hiking trip, less than a week after they'd met. They had exchanged telephone numbers at the last moment. Thursday evening, Afsaneh called Ramin's house and he answered the phone. They arranged to go to Darakeh.

"Yesterday when I called you, if someone else had answered, I wouldn't have known what to do."

"You might have hung up."

"No, I wouldn't have. I wanted to talk to you. But I didn't know what to say. I'm not one of those people who can lie easily."

"Perhaps you haven't been taught."

"I haven't had many people around me."

Her father, Samad Khan, was sitting on the verandah with his plastered leg on a lamp table. Ozra brought the fire brazier to the yard, and four or five-year-old Afsaneh followed Ozra, crying. She was looking for Sara, but her mother wasn't home. Afsaneh hadn't seen her for a while. She wasn't home yesterday either. She might not have been home for weeks. Afsaneh wanted Sara. Ozra was impatient. She held Afsaneh's hand and took her to the pond. The big pond was in the middle of the yard and the shadows of the trees danced on the pond. Goldfish swam side by side, as if narrating tales for each other or talking about their sorrows.

"Be a good girl," Ozra said, "stay here and watch the goldfish. If the black cat wants to hunt them, shoo it away."

Ozra caressed her hair, but not the way Sara did. Sara sat Afsaneh on her lap and Afsaneh could smell her perfume, a perfume she recognized from other places and other times. Samad Khan rested his broken leg like a log on a lamp table and had a book open, humming. He drank a red-coloured drink from a tall glass. Afsaneh wanted to drink it, too. Samad Khan lifted the glass to her mouth, but its harsh smell and its bitter taste made her run away. She went to the yard, then followed Ozra to the basement and asked for Sara.

Afsaneh didn't know when Sara left. She hadn't seen her leave. She only felt her absence in the house. When Sara wasn't home, the silence in the house deepened. Ozra was in a bad mood. Samad Khan sent Afsaneh away, and if she stayed beside him, he would offer her his foul smelling drink and she'd flee. The house was in mourning. The trees, birds, fish, even the cobblestones in the yard were silent in Sara's absence. Afsaneh sat on the first step of the stairs and watched the afternoon disappearing. Her pestering and crying made Ozra impatient. A few days ago Ozra had said the black cat was hunting one of fish, the one who had a big belly, full of thousands of baby fish. Every afternoon Afsaneh sat by the pond with Ozra, and Ozra showed her the fish one by one, calling them names Afsaneh couldn't remember. Watching the fish, Afsaneh turned her head to every sound that could be Sara. She knew that when Sara was back, the house would be full of joy. Ozra had told her Sara would show up any moment. The master was worried too, and when the master was worried, Ozra was in a bad mood and behaved badly.

Two goldfish swam side-by-side, opening and closing their mouths, as if talking about happiness. Afsaneh saw the black cat perched under a tree among the bushes. She was anxious for the fish, and didn't take her eyes off the cat. While she watched the fish swimming slowly and carelessly at the edge of the pond, a crow sat in a tree cawing loudly, spreading its shadow on the pond. The fish plunged into the water and then surfaced, flapping their fins and closing their mouths. The black cat didn't move, it half opened an eye and closed it again. Afsaneh watched the fish swimming at the edge of the pond side by side. Another crow broke the silence with sharp cawing and sat on a short branch. One crow flew down to the water's surface. Flapping split the air. Afsaneh saw goldfish flying in the air in the crow's beak. She rushed at the crow and fell into the pond. She heard Sara's voice, screaming and catching her. When she came to herself, Afsaneh saw the sky overhead, and Sara's eyes staring at her, wrapping her in kindness. She took Afsaneh to the verandah. Sara changed the child's dress and spoke harshly to Samad Khan and Ozra. She kissed Afsaneh again and hugged her. Sara's lovely smell was in her nostrils again.

That was the beginning of her childhood, the beginning of memory. Afsaneh didn't remember anything before that incident. She remembered afternoons, sitting with Ozra by the pond. The house empty, Ozra talking about the pond mother who lived at the bottom of the pond. She talked about genies hidden in corners of the house, in the basement, and at the bottom of the pond. They would have feasts, dancing and singing in the yard when it was dark. Ozra's tales never finished, the tales were told once, and if Afsaneh asked for the black hoof genie once more, and if Ozra told it once again, it would be different. Told again, the black genie didn't have hooves, or didn't hunt beautiful girls. It was white and lived in a jungle.

Then the pond was replaced by a swimming pool. The dark water changed to blue, like the colour of sky. The pool was big. Sara in a red swimsuit, and Samad Khan half-naked, were in the water. Sara held Afsaneh over the surface of the water and told her to move her hands and her legs to swim. Then they put a plastic tube around her chest and left her floating on the water. On sunny days, she was in the water the whole day with that plastic tube around her waist. The fish moved to a small pond with blue walls. While she was in the pool, she watched cats and crows, and if a crow sat on a tree branch, she called Ozra, or Sara if she was home.

Later on, Sara went away and didn't come back. Samad Khan, too. She remembered the day Samad Khan left. Her grandmother wailed. Samad Khan's photo lay on the ground. Afsaneh found out about death that day, but it was years before she finally knew what had happened to Sara. When she was older, Ozra told her. Sara was killed in an accident.

Afsaneh remembered their house was filled with people wearing black. Men and women. She remembered all that blackness, and her grandmother's lament. They kept her in the back room, and she smelled Sara's perfume everywhere. Samad Khan's absence wasn't important. After Sara left and didn't come back, her father hadn't been home. Ozra told her later that he was repeatedly found drunk and unconscious in taverns and brought home. He finally died of his deep sorrow.

Ozra told her, Samad Khan was your mother's lover. He was a dervish, a hermit who never cared about material things or having an ordinary way of life. Your mother brought him back to the house. He was devoted to your mother, but your mother didn't appreciate him, her thoughts were elsewhere. God forgive me, it is a sin to say so, but your mother wasn't faithful to him. Perhaps because Samad Khan was very much older than her, old enough to be her father. But he was a gentleman. He was a hundred times better than the men today.

"Sometimes I think I didn't have a childhood, and if I had, I don't remember it. After my father's death I remember some things. We moved to Tehran and I lived with my grandmother and attended school, a boring life, with my grandmother and Ozra. We lived in an old house in Sarchemeh, one of the old neighbourhoods in Tehran. The house had many big rooms, basements, and a pond in the middle of the yard which reminded me of the pond in our big house in Varamin. I remember my grandmother very well. I was fifteen when she died. To tell the truth, her death didn't bother me. I didn't cry. I didn't love her, because I sensed she didn't love me. I heard her call me a witch. I couldn't understand what she meant by that, but in her eyes and her voice I could feel she didn't love me. Whether I was there or not was the same for her. So for me, too, it was the same. She didn't matter. When she died, I felt pity for her, but I forgot her quickly. Ozra, I loved. She was my whole family. Sometimes she punished me, beat me, when I was younger. Not very hard, but she did. When I cried, she hugged me, kissed me and gave me candies or cookies. She smelled of fried onion, burnt wood, and soap. I liked her smell. She was stout with big breasts. I felt secure when she took me in her arms. She told me strange tales. About genies, red ones, green genies, horned genies, hoofed genies. My grandmother never told me a story. When I was nine years old, she tried to teach me how to pray. I never learned. I lied to her. 'I've done my prayers,' I'd say, and she didn't care. I think she viewed me as belonging to my mother, rather than as her grandchild.

"Obviously, I was a thorn in her heart. But what could I do? I was a burden she couldn't ignore. She rarely took me anywhere. I was always at home, wandering beside Ozra as she told me tales. She talked about her daughter who had green eyes, like Ozra's eyes. She didn't know what happened to her daughter. She said the genies had taken her away. The girl had been with her for just a week. She remembered her green eyes, and called her Hoorie, Angel. She talked about Hoorie as if she had raised her. My grandmother said that was nonsense. She told me Ozra became pregnant by someone else, and claimed that both my uncles were her baby's father."

"When I was older, Ozra told me both of them slept with her. Sometimes Samad Khan, and sometimes Majid Khan. And sometimes their father. She said the three of them were her baby's father."

"Three of them? Is it possible?"

"Yes, it is."

"Grandmother said, 'Majid Khan was in France. He left Iran when he was eighteen, and didn't come back for years. Samad Khan was never at home, and Agha died when Ozra was a child.'"

I said, "Majid Khan, who is the father of Ozra's child?"

"Don't interfere," he said, "when Ozra got pregnant, I was in France. And your father didn't care about women. She was an easy-going girl. God knows with whom she slept, and then she claimed her child was from our family. It was Mother's fault, keeping her in our home with her big belly. She wanted to marry her to Sayed Morad, whose wife had become paralyzed. But the man wouldn't have her with a bastard child."

"What happened to the child then?"

"A family adopted her. And Ozra went to the hospital to have her tubes tied."

"Did she still go with other men?"

"How do I know? Mother believed she wasn't careful enough and her belly might fill again."

I told Ozra, "Think about it. This isn't Hoorie. Hoorie would be older, older than Aida. Aida is just twenty-years-old and her mother is French."

Ozra stared at me with her green eyes. When she was angry, black threads appeared in her eyes. Her voice became hoarse and broken. She screamed, "It's her. Isn't her father Majid Khan? Aren't her eyes green? This is my Hoorie, they stole and took to France."

"But Aida has another mother."

"How do you know that woman gave birth to Hoorie?"

"Aida isn't Hoorie," I said.

That summer, Aida had traveled to Iran with her father, Majid Khan. They were supposed to stay with us for two months. Since Grandmother died, Majid Khan spent his summers in Iran to see me and to manage the land and buildings he had inherited from his father. There were two big houses on Jaleh Street which were my bequest from my late father. Majid Khan destroyed them and built apartment buildings instead. At the same time he did some surgery in one of Tehran's hospitals. His temperament was the opposite of my father's. He was always looking for ways to make money.

We sat in the yard. Ozra had spread a rug by the pond, and I studied for my final high school exams, though at that moment I was paying more attention to sparrows chirping happily. The sky was a deep blue. The trees were quiet, their leaves whispering to the breeze. I was far away from my textbooks and exams, thinking about Ozra's claim. When I told her she'd better be logical, forget her childish thoughts, she looked at me like she was thinking deeply, as if she might have to make a terrible decision. She threw away a sandwich she had made for me. She reached to do the same with the dish of watermelon too, but I stopped her hand.

"Very well, you're right. Assume Aida is your Hoorie, what then?"

Without listening to me, she went to the basement and didn't come out until late at night.

Ozra was my companion. She is woven into every memory I have from childhood. I wanted to take her with me to France. I'd made all the arrangements. Majid Khan made fun of me, "You're like a landowner, fifty years ago, you want to take your nanny with you."

"Majid Khan, Ozra isn't my nanny. She's my whole family. I was raised by Ozra. I can't live without her, nor she without me."

He laughed, ridiculing me and said, "You really are your father's child. A vein of his madness is in you."

"Tell me about my father. How did he fall in love with my mother? She was so much younger than him, sixteen when he was forty-four."

"Both were crazy," he said, "and you are the product of two crazy people. God save you."

"I don't remember whether my father loved me," I said, "I never saw any kindness from him. But, you love Aida."

"Your father was mad about your mother," he said, "he didn't love anyone except your mother."

"Even his own child?"

"What do you expect from a madman?"

I didn't tell him I wanted to be like my father, to be in love like him, and devote my whole life to love.

The sky over the mountains was pure blue. Faraway, towards the city, faded to gray. The city stretched out under a cloud of smoke, and the setting sun in the west lit the highest section of mountains. The wind was cold on her face, which was tinged by sunlight. A sweet anxiety in her heart forced her to talk to Ramin incessantly. She was enchanted to have someone to talk with. One time, she woke up at dawn and listened to the silence. Her window was open and the morning breeze blew in. She asked herself, "Am I in love?" and heard her answer, "yes."

Whenever she heard the telephone ring, she smiled and said to herself, "Is it Ramin?" And if it wasn't him, she felt cold. Words stuck to her tongue. She finished the telephone call indifferently, and waited for the phone to ring again.

When Ramin did call, her heart beat faster, her cheeks became hot, and her hands went cold. She talked quickly, laughed without reason, and asked for a date.

"If before meeting you, I had heard about you, known about your life, the child of a landowning father with an inheritance large enough to live on without working, I wouldn't believe it."

"What? Do I have horns and hooves? Did I descend from the trunk of an elephant?"

"Something like that."

"It was good that you knew me first, and then found out about my background."

"I wonder why you came back from France?"

"You mean I should have stayed there? Everywhere you go the sky is the same colour."

"The sky, yes. But we live on earth."

"My problem is life on earth. I couldn't assimilate. Perhaps our cultural differences wouldn't let me. And I knew French people, they didn't treat me badly. They found out I was from a wealthy family, as you say a landowning family, even though I didn't talk about myself. They asked many questions until they realized I'd lost my parents in childhood. Then they sympathized with me and imagined I was raised in an orphanage. I explained everything and they asked, "Why did you come to France?" Then when I explained I had a wealthy father, they changed their opinion of me. It was always the same. So I couldn't be comfortable. Everybody I got to know wanted to know about my family. I couldn't just be friends with a French person without questions and answers. I could spend some time with them, that was it. Perhaps our past created a gulf between us. We didn't have shared memories, we didn't have things in common. If I stayed longer I would probably have become used to them, and then I couldn't come back here. But I was waiting to finish my studies and return. Then there was the revolution, and many came back. I couldn't stay away either. But those few years were a chance for me to learn the French language, and with French I could find a job."

"But you don't need to work."

"Even though I don't need to work, I still prefer to work and pay my expenses."

"So you're an exceptional landowner."

"Maybe, maybe not. By the time I found out I was a landowner, my dear uncle had already taken most of my wealth."

"What is left is enough for your whole life."

"But I don't think about these things."

"Do you think about starvation?"

"What about you?"

"I think about people who are starving."

"Me, too."

"And you do nothing."

"What should I do?"

"You know about the class struggle, don't you?"

"You mean the struggle between rich and poor?"

"Something like that. I would like to know, which class do you defend?"

"Me? I haven't thought about it. Why should I be involved in this struggle?"

"You are involved in it, whether you want to be or not. All of us are involved in it. We defend either the rich or the poor. Which side are you on?"

She didn't answer.

"Huh? Why don't you answer? Obviously, you defend your own class."

"I'm thinking like Hafiz, 'The wrangle of seventy-two sects establishes excuse for all, When truth, they saw not, the door to the fable they beat'."

"But this is not a fable, it's reality."

Ramin spoke about the struggle of workers throughout history. He spoke about workers' rights, about social class, about socialist countries. She was amazed. His words were just words. They didn't touch her, didn't make any impression on her.

Afsaneh heard footsteps coming close to her. Her breath caught in her chest, her heart beat violently. Is it him? Yes, it is. She recognized his footsteps, hurried and fast. Coming closer. She closed her eyes and imagined him. I hoped he would come back and he did. The sound came closer. The footsteps echoed in her heart, made it pound faster. When the sound was close, she stood and opened her eyes. A man Ramin's height, in a gray sweatshirt, stopped in front of her tent, said a word of greeting, and started to jog again. A breeze set her shivering. She felt cold and went back to sit on the bench. The taste of hope stayed with her for a few minutes, the belief he might come back. When he left, hope had sat down beside her. "He'll be back, he won't leave me alone."

"What are you going to do?"

"Stay here."

"Alone?"

She didn't answer. She poked the dying fire with a twig and scattered the ashes in the air.

"Let's go. Don't be so stubborn."

She didn't answer.

"Afsaneh, accept it, don't behave like a child. These few days are enough for our whole lives."

She looked at Ramin and said nothing. Let him go, she thought. She couldn't keep on. She couldn't beg him. She absolutely could not beg. She had never begged for anything from anyone. She had never learned how to. And he was right, begging wouldn't work. He had decided to ignore what he really wanted. He had responsibilities and she did not. Ramin had commitment on his shoulders and would devote himself to his responsibilities. Who was she? An offspring of landowners with no worries. Yes, she was the problem. Perhaps, as Ramin was saying, she didn't understand. Why should she understand? Why did she hang on to Ramin? Hadn't she lived without him, all these years? She could do it again. Could she? She thought about tomorrow.

"Tomorrow?"

Tomorrow was too far away.

"Tomorrow I'll go hiking with a group. If you'd like to spend time with us you can come too."

"Why do you insist on drawing a line between me and yourself and making a class distinction? Aren't the hikers human beings? If they're like you and me, I can mix with them, don't worry. I would like to meet with your group, find out about your ideas."

"I think you should understand what our ideas are."

"I've found out more or less, but to me words aren't important. All talk."

"What do you think should be done?"

"I have no idea."

Talk of social issues didn't interest her. She refused to answer Ramin, who spoke like a student, with a memorized speech on all subjects. She became impatient and didn't know what to say. She asked herself, what's wrong with me? Is it me who doesn't understand or... She said involuntarily, "I'm the child of landowners without any worries. The class struggle means nothing to me."

That stopped Ramin. But beyond these discussions and arguments, she and Ramin had an attraction to each other. Whenever they arranged to meet, she was anxious he might not come. Up to the last moment, she thought politics and class might separate them. Then when she and Ramin met, she knew words meant nothing; she knew they needed each other. Before meeting the group for hiking, she thought they might be a bunch of young dreamers, thinking they could change the world into paradise with words.

That day, she couldn't believe a sixteen-year-old girl on the verge of becoming an adult could snatch Ramin out of her hands by tricking him, and take him away. So far away that she had to forget him, forget even thinking about him. The girl walked quickly between Ramin and Siamak, as they came up to her Renault. Afsaneh was waiting for them, on a spring morning in Tajrish Square. Just before they reached her, she stepped out of her car, stretched her hand towards Ramin, and shook his hand warmly. Perhaps she was aware of a vague danger. At their first meeting she couldn't see that Ramin had any love for his cousin. Later on, he told her their mothers considered them destined to be wife and husband. His mother always called Negar her daughter-in-law.

Siamak was more friendly than Negar. He was as tall as Ramin, and similar to his sister, with his pale complexion, brown eyes, and corn-coloured hair. He was excitable. Ramin told her Siamak was three years older than he was, but he looked younger. Ramin, with his quiet character and questioning gaze seemed wiser and more mature than Siamak. But Siamak's joyfulness, his talkative, restless personality was attractive. He had a fire inside and wanted to enflame everybody with that fire. A few months later, when he was arrested, Afsaneh knew his fire would consume him.

She and Ramin later talked a lot about Siamak, before and after he was arrested. Ramin's enthusiasm about Siamak was obvious when he spoke. She wanted to warn him that fervent disciples can lose their way, but she couldn't. Obviously, the whole group she met hiking were just beginning to learn about the world and to experience life.

The day she went hiking she realized that each one in the group wanted to prove to the others that he or she was the bravest. She was the odd one out. The whole day she climbed with them, but refused to join in their discussion. She still didn't know what she wanted. She just watched Ramin, burning inside with her fire. He seemed boisterous and happy compared to other times she'd seen him. Whenever they met each other's eyes, a shadow of sadness crossed hers, as if they were saying to each other, "What are we doing here?" Negar walked close to Ramin and talked to him.

While hiking, Afsaneh realized she had misjudged Negar. Negar wasn't a child. Even with her youth and immature body, she knew more than Afsaneh about how to trick and charm the opposite sex. Negar didn't leave Ramin alone for any length of time. On these last few days camping, Ramin admitted Negar had made a decision at the beginning of the day to stand between Ramin and Afsaneh and not let them be together. Perhaps Negar realized quickly that the link between Afsaneh and Ramin wasn't a simple friendship. She understood Afsaneh wasn't just "a landowner friend" as Ramin had described her to Siamak. Negar noticed the love in Afsaneh's eyes. A few months later, when Ramin came to her place with Negar, and Afsaneh learned he had married her to help her escape across the border, she knew she had misunderstood Negar, underestimated her shrewdness.

Two or three hours after they started hiking, Negar fell and pretended her leg was hurt. She called Ramin, who was walking ahead of the group with Afsaneh. She kept him beside her until they returned.

"It's late. He has left me and won't come back. Night is spreading darkness everywhere. Spreading darkness over my head and drowning me in it. Why am I waiting? I know he won't be back. If I hadn't been so optimistic, if I had bound him to me as Negar did, I wouldn't be obliged to beg for my share of happiness now. That woman stole my happiness back then, and she's stealing it again now. Didn't he promise last night he'd never leave me? Didn't he tell me he hadn't lived until today? Didn't he say he came back to life in these few nights? Why, then, did he leave me? Commitment? Responsibilities? I don't believe him. Isn't love above all of these things? He's in love with me. I know he is. He'll be back. He'll be back for sure."

The spreading shadow deepened and darkened. And she was still sitting on the bench, stuck in place, like a piece of wood. She was disturbed, swimming in the air, weightless and without sensation.

"He left me. I lost him, again. I lost him once before. After only a few months. Three? Four? Six months? That time, before Siamak was arrested. Then I could have slept with him and bound him to me. That cold, dark night when Tehran was bombed, and he stayed with me.

"What do you usually do?"
"I stay here in the dark."
"Aren't you afraid?"

"Of course I'm afraid, it isn't possible not to be afraid. When I see death pouring from the sky, how is it possible not to be afraid?"

"Why don't you go to the basement? It would offer some shelter."

"Yes, it's a shelter. But if I'm meant to die in a bombing raid, I'd prefer to die alone inside my home. Among those crowds who take refuge in that basement, fear kills more quickly than bombs."

"Fear is hard to control. Life is dear."

"Yes, I know. And it's still true, even if it's said a million times. My life is as dear to me as theirs is to them. But I'm not afraid of darkness, I'm afraid of bombs. Those people are afraid of darkness."

They were standing by the window of Afsaneh's apartment. The night, deep and dark, the chilly breeze of fall, then sudden death descending from the sky spread fear to every corner of the apartment. When the bombing was over, the city filled with the haunting urgency of ambulance sirens. Afsaneh talked non-stop to prevent her real feelings from showing.

"A foolish pride. Foolish pride and I don't know where it came from. Why did I hide my real feelings? Instead of speaking non-sense, why didn't I say how I felt? Why did I talk rubbish and act cowardly?"

She could rest her hand on his, she could stare into his eyes, without uttering one word, without telling him she loved him, with their mouths full of promises, joined by their love.

"What happened to me? To my courage? Why didn't I pay attention to my heart, beating hard in my chest? Why didn't I let him hear my heart and know how much I loved and needed him? Why didn't I tell him that since the first moment we met I felt a closeness? Why didn't I let him speak? Anytime a silence fell between us, I talked, not letting him open his mouth. He might have had something to say. He might have felt the same."

"Do you remember? I'm talking about that night, the night of the bombing when I was in your place. I stayed overnight. I decided to come to your room several times, and every time I told myself, what if she doesn't want me? What if it's just a dream? I told myself, if you loved me, you would have said so. You seemed like a strong woman who got what you wanted. I didn't deserve your love. I felt inferior to you. Not because you were two years older than me. You were very mature, worldly-wise. And I was like a student. I felt protected by you. I told myself: I have to live under your protective shadow forever. It scared and captivated me. That night your love became unachievable for me. If I hadn't stayed overnight at your place, perhaps I would have spoken of my love. But that night, you became like an unconquerable castle. I told myself, she is not like us, like ordinary people. Someone special deserves her love. That's how you seemed to me."

Afsaneh missed her chance. Later, when Ramin came to her place with a marriage ring on his finger, she tried to act as if nothing had happened. Each time she went to the kitchen to fetch something, she swallowed her tears and then returned to the living room. Ramin stared at her and she was bewildered. Once, when she was away too long, Negar came into the kitchen. Afsaneh opened the fridge door and busied herself. Whether Ramin realized what she was feeling, she didn't know.

"I noticed nothing. You were on edge, but I didn't know why. How would I know?"

"It was my mistake. A foolish pride separated us, and I slept with that other man as soon as he proposed to me."

"What do you mean when you look at me in that way? Have I done something wrong?"

"Wrong? No, no I don't mean that."

"You asked me and I accepted, so we are husband and wife. Why wait for a clergyman to make it legal? Don't kisses seal the marriage?"

"What an interesting idea!"

"I wasn't in love with him, but I didn't dislike him, either. After all, I had to marry. He didn't seem to be a bad man. He was physically similar to you, especially his face and height. Perhaps that similarity deceived me. For a few months, he followed me with his eyes. His cousin, Sussan, told me he liked me. Well, I couldn't stay alone all my life. I was twenty-eight. I wanted to have a family, something I never had. I wanted to have children, I wanted to get pregnant. I had a need for a child — a need I couldn't deny. I slept with him the first night he asked me to marry him. Do you understand? Men weren't scarce, but I couldn't be with just any man. It wasn't easy for me. I fled from all of them. Everyone I met, I compared with you. I liked Bahram. He was similar to you. Sometimes, when I saw him entering a room, I thought I saw you and my heart fluttered. Then I told myself, I'd grow old waiting for you. I wasn't young any more. I became impatient. I imagined that with Bahram, I might get my vitality back. I imagined I might get pregnant. I wanted two or three children of my own. I wanted to experience a childhood, which I didn't remember, revive it with my own children. That didn't happen either. Bahram deceived me. He didn't tell me the truth. I never forgave him. He claimed it was my fault he hid the truth from me. He wasn't someone who would talk about his past. He was surprised I was a virgin. He said, 'Why? No one was controlling you. You spent a few years in France, you could have enjoyed your life.' You see, he thought that way. What could I expect from that man? His past was shameful. When I heard what he had done, that he got rid of that girl for a thousand dollars to obey his father, I hated him. He howled like a dog and begged me not to leave him. But I couldn't stay with him. I couldn't live with such a worthless man. His love seemed cheap to me. I left him. I realized why he hated children. Why he didn't want to adopt a child. You see, I missed you. For two years and five months I lived with a man like that. Do you think I was happy away from you?"

I was happy these last few nights and days. Perhaps that is all the happiness that's coming to me. Perhaps I shouldn't expect more. Perhaps I shouldn't complain. Forget all those years, keep these days and nights. Forget the years when I didn't know Ramin, the years when I was far away from him. And these last two years close to him but still separate. Two years worse than all the previous ones. Close to him but I couldn't touch him. I saw his suffering and couldn't do anything, couldn't soothe him. If he hadn't left his house, if he hadn't come to me, if these nights never happened, what would I have to be happy about? Why was I born?"

"Why was I born? Why did my mother give birth to me? Why, when she delivered me, didn't she kill me? A bastard! Why did she give me to a stranger?"

"My daughter's eyes were green. I called her Hoorie, 'angel'. All God's angels have green eyes."

"My dear Afsaneh, take care of my Hoorie. If you find her, tell her I always remembered her, tell her. Don't forget."

Afsaneh wanted to take Ozra to France with her, but Ozra became ill. A high fever and hallucinations. Majid Khan examined her and said, "Meningitis, she should be hospitalized." Afsaneh stayed with her four days and nights. On the fifth day Afsaneh came home, took a shower and lay down. She fell asleep, woke the next morning and rushed to the hospital to see a body under a white sheet. She went to Ozra and pulled aside the sheet.

"She died an hour ago," the nurse told her.

"Didn't she ask for me?"

"No, she just called for Hoorie."

Ozra's face seemed younger. She looked asleep. The wrinkles around her mouth and eyes had disappeared.

Afsaneh was waiting at her apartment door after answering her bell, expecting a man and woman to come out of the elevator. When she saw a young woman climbing to the tenth floor up the staircase, she was shocked. It was as if she was finally seeing Ozra's daughter. "Hoorie," she uttered involuntarily.

The woman was followed by a man of almost forty, tiny, with a few days growth of beard, wearing a black collarless shirt, eyes red from heat or fatigue and a sulky face. She invited them into the apartment, asked them to sit down, and sat in front of them, wondering why they had come. The man initiated the conversation.

"This woman is the daughter of your maid, Ozra, and an illegitimate child of Majid Khan or Samad Khan. She should be considered your cousin or your sister."

If Afsaneh had been told that Ozra had left her grave, and had come to visit, she couldn't have been more surprised than when she saw Hoorie. She had believed in Hoorie, when Ozra was alive, but with Ozra's death, Hoorie disappeared from her mind too. She said involuntarily, "Hoorie?"

With rude, hateful gestures the man said, "Not Hoorie. Firoozeh. Her name is Firoozeh."

"But Ozra always said her daughter's name was Hoorie."

"My uncle and his wife called her Firoozeh. Her name on her birth certificate is Firoozeh as well."

He took out a faded piece of paper from his waist pocket, unfolded it and read it to Afsaneh. *Nosrat and Mahmood Seraji adopt the newborn Ozra's daughter as their child, and Ozra has no right to ask for her daughter under any condition.* There was a faded fingerprint at the bottom of the paper.

The man folded the paper and put it in his pocket again, staring with his bold eyes at Afsaneh, saying, "You see, Khanum. This woman, Hoorie, as you call her, is an illegitimate child of poor Ozra."

The woman, who had been quiet all the time, asked, "Where is she?"

"Who?" Afsaneh asked dumbfounded.

"Ozra, my mother."

"She passed away. A few years ago. She died of meningitis."

Firoozeh's desolate face brought tears to Afsaneh's eyes. Firoozeh, too, wiped tears with her chador.

The man said, "Khanum, everyone dies. Everybody will die one day. But that woman shouldn't have abandoned her own daughter. She should have pleaded for justice. She should have gotten her rights from the Afsharnia family. They had millions and they still do. You seem to have some of that wealth. Khanum, I live in two rented rooms in Majidieh, with three girls and a pregnant wife. And you, aren't you sisters or at least cousins?"

"I know nothing," Afsaneh said, "I wasn't born at that time."

"Yes, you're right. The sin rests on your father's or your uncle's shoulders. But you can claim your sister's right."

She mumbled, "My sister!"

Day had disappeared and night fallen. Afsaneh lit the lamp, served watermelon and tea twice. The man still talked. He talked about hardships, about revolution, about Islam, revealing his devotion to Imam Khomeini. He convicted Majid Khan and Samad Khan without knowing them. He called them servants of America and the Shah, and threatened to take them to court.

Afsaneh said, "My father is dead, and Majid Khan lives in France."

The man was dumbfounded for a minute. Then he said, "Their belongings aren't dead. Land is God's and never dies."

Afsaneh heard the irony. "If I can help, I will. Ozra was like a mother to me."

Afsaneh explained she had lost her parents when she was five years old, and Ozra had raised her. She considered Ozra blood family. She told them she would take one of her Jaleh Street apartments back from the tenant and allow them to live there.

Asad quieted down. But he still threatened her family and talked about God and the Islamic court. When the power went out, Asad's eyes opened wide, "Is it an air attack?"

There was no siren or sound of anti-aircraft. He relaxed. Afsaneh gave them a ride to their home. On their way she was stuck in heavy traffic, and the intersection was blocked. Asad changed to complaints about the war, the system and anarchy.

Darkness spread everywhere. There was a vague rustling in the trees. A bear? Afsaneh rose automatically and went into the tent, closing the zipper. She threw herself on the sleeping bag and sobbed, burying her face into the sleeping bag to stifle the sound. Her body trembled and shivered with cold. "He left me. He left. He left."

"Tomorrow I'll talk to him."

The next day she didn't see him. She called his house several times. Maziar said he wasn't home. When will he be back? He said he didn't know. Afsaneh stood by the window and watched the night coming, invading Yousefabad Street.

"Where has he gone? We were supposed to see each other today. I have to tell him. I can't wait any longer. And if he doesn't love me… A landowner's daughter." A smile appeared on her face.

"If all landowners were like you."

"And if you didn't draw a line between us."

Sometimes she woke in the middle of the night and listened to the silence. She stayed awake for hours asking herself, what happened to me? She saw Ramin in the darkness, imagined him beside her, talked to him and asked, "You too?" Her heart beat harder. She told herself, tomorrow, tomorrow when I see him, I'll tell him.

Then when she saw him, Ramin didn't let her talk. He talked about persecution and arrests. Anger shadowed his words and his behaviour, smothered the words in her. Ramin was worried about Siamak, that Siamak's life was in danger. Afsaneh had to stop herself. It wasn't a good time to talk about love.

It was drizzling. The darkness at seven o'clock in the evening and the sound of rain hitting the window panes reminded her of when Ozra was alive. Afsaneh, busy with her homework and Ozra knitting socks for herself. The socks she had started to knit at the beginning of the cold season and hadn't finished by the end of winter. Afsaneh daydreamed, a book open on her knee, her attention on the window and the rain. A rootless anxiety took hold of her. The central heat wasn't on yet. Her apartment was cold, she had a blanket across her knees. The damp cold of the rain penetrated the closed window. She stared at the window.

The telephone rang and she sprang from her place. Recognizing Ramin's voice, her heart pounded madly in her chest.

"I want to come over there and talk to you. I know it's late, but I have to see you."

She had a bottle of wine in the fridge, she didn't remember how long she had kept it. She lit a candle on the table and went into her bedroom. She sat by the mirror to make herself up. She put on her light green shirt. Her eyes gleamed and she felt a quiver of ecstasy that made her anxious.

Seconds passed as if stuck to the face of the clock. She turned the ceiling lamp off, left the kitchen lamp on. The candle on the table spread a delicate trembling light. Her living room, with prints by Monet, Van Gogh, and Gaugin, souvenirs from Paris museums, lace curtains and a pale green rug, had a new meaning.

"Why so much green?"

"The colour of Ozra and Hoorie's eyes."

"Hoorie? Ozra's imaginary daughter?"

"Yes, Ozra's imaginary daughter she never found."

The wailing of cars, trucks and buses gradually faded and the city became quiet. Ten o'clock and no sign of Ramin. The candle burned out. Afsaneh wanted to light another one, but didn't. Disappointment replaced joy. "He's playing with me."

The doorbell made her jump. She rushed to the intercom, heard Ramin's familiar voice and relaxed. She remembered her enthusiasm an hour ago and wanted to light a candle but it was too late. There was knock at the apartment door. She turned on the lamp and opened the door. Ramin and Siamak were at her door. She invited them in, and forgot about the wine.

"Just for a few days, until he can find another safe place."

Siamak stayed. Ramin left.

Those few days passed in a nightmare of discussion with Siamak. Siamak defended his beliefs stubbornly, and sometimes without listening to what Afsaneh said. Afsaneh thought his beliefs were prejudiced and narrow-minded. In France, she had met many students who thought and behaved like Siamak. Many of them were fascinated by ideas they didn't understand correctly. When she noticed contradictions between their beliefs and their actions, she turned her back on them.

Siamak was different. Siamak was Ramin's saint, his leader, and a man of knowledge. His words and his ideas were accepted by Ramin without question. Perhaps because she thought he was idolized by Ramin and his other friends, she had set herself against him from the beginning. Even when she agreed with him, she still didn't want to accept his point. As if she had decided to reveal another side of this admired idol to prove he was an ordinary person like everyone else. Perhaps she was jealous of Siamak. Ramin worshipped him. Perhaps she considered him a barrier to her love.

Afsaneh disagreed with Siamak's ideas; he stubbornly defended them. He ignored her, sneeringly mocked her, labeled her as from a class which was against the workers and against him. Afsaneh did the same. Battle was waged between them. She didn't answer his questions, pretended she wasn't listening. She laughed at his ideas, sang a song and ignored him. She told herself, "I hate their so-called workers. It's not clear that he or his father is a worker. I can defend the peasant class, too. Words are cheap."

That day their discussion started about nothing in particular. Afsaneh noticed she couldn't stand up to Siamak's stinging and ironic remarks. She couldn't force him to listen to her, so she became quiet. She was bored with his presence in her home, but didn't want to hurt him. Ramin wouldn't forgive her. Even the brief friendship they had would be over. She went to the kitchen to make lunch. Standing by the stove, she was busy preparing food. Through the window she could see the mountains of Darakeh, last night's delicate snow melting in the sunshine. The smell of wet soil and fallen leaves, the silence in the air and the blue of the sky, held a sense of sadness. She was humming a song by Elaheh. She sensed the presence of Siamak in the kitchen, and ignored him.

"I didn't know you had a nice voice," Siamak said.

She stopped singing, busy with her work.

"Continue. You sing beautifully."

With a little smile she continued to sing. Her back was to him, she was busy cooking, concentrating on her song. Siamak came close to her and hugged her. She jumped as if she received an electric shock. She looked at him harshly. Siamak smiled back still holding her in his arms. Afsaneh separated from him and left the kitchen. Closing her bedroom door, she stayed there thinking for a while. Then she put on her head scarf and left the apartment.

They were in a restaurant in the Shemiran area. Afsaneh chose it because Ramin was now under suspicion. The dining room was semi-dark, lit by candles on tables and weak lamps. Afsaneh wore a gray jacket with a black skirt. She had on her colourful Torkaman scarf which covered part of her hair and shoulders, and gave her the appearance of a wealthy woman. Ramin had a suit on, and a white shirt without a tie, unbuttoned at the collar. They'd chosen a table at the far end of the restaurant under a dim light. Afsaneh ordered roast chicken for herself. Ramin said he didn't have much appetite, he would just have a salad.

"Don't be childish again. I'm sure you're worrying about the money. I told you, don't worry. It'll be my treat."

"Okay. I agree. I'm always defenseless against you. To tell the truth I haven't eaten lunch either. These days..."

"Please don't start again. Let's have our meal in peace."

There was silence, except that Siamak was between them. Afsaneh's thoughts turned toward Siamak without her willing it. She knew Ramin was doing the same. It was the first time they had been together since Siamak had left her place. The silence length-ened, words refused to flow from their tongues. Afsaneh looked around. The restaurant was quiet weekdays, but she didn't pay at-tention to her surroundings, busy with her own thoughts. She waited for Ramin to say something. She knew he would talk about Siamak. Then she could defend herself.

"He told me he didn't mean to," Ramin said, "he didn't have any control. It was an instinctive desire."

The waiter put a large bowl of salad on the table and left. Afsaneh served a plate of salad for herself, adding lemon juice and olive oil to it. She pushed the salad bowl to Ramin and said, "I can't believe it. Instinctive! Only animals can't control their in-stincts."

Ramin put some salad on his plate. "Human beings are partly animal, too. Why are you so hard on him? Now that he's arrested, you have to forget about it."

She took a piece of lettuce with her fork and put it in her mouth, staring at Ramin, saying, "I'm not hard on him. I'm not thinking about it either. But a person like him! He wore out my patience. He didn't value anyone except himself. Because I didn't think like him, he didn't value my ideas and didn't listen to me. He considered himself from a special race and special species. He was born to rescue the workers and the workers can't survive without him. Then, there was his behaviour."

"I don't see any abnormality in his behaviour. He's a man. No matter how he's thinking or what his beliefs, he's still a man. He can't deny his desire, the same desires we all have."

"But he claims he is going to rescue humanity."

"He might have not seen the contradiction."

"Only people like Siamak don't see contradictions between their behaviour and their beliefs. I hope you don't think like him. At least, don't behave like him."

The waiter placed roast chicken in front of Afsaneh and a plate of *chello kebab* in front of Ramin, standing until Afsaneh motioned him away with a nod.

Without touching his food, Ramin said, "Me? To tell the truth, I still don't know exactly what I think. I still..."

"Perhaps you're confused."

"Yes, I'm confused."

"You're bewitched by Siamak. You look at him as if he's a saint."

"Yes, he is. I confess, I admire him. People like him…"

He added a dash of sumac to his kebab and put a spoon of food into his mouth, staring at Afsaneh, who had a piece of chicken in her hand.

"So we probably have many saints. Tell me which ones should we worship?"

"Not worship. The question is their faith. They sacrifice themselves for their faith."

"Faith in what?"

"Faith in a holy goal."

"My problem is with that goal. I've noticed more hate in them than holy goal. Hate for anybody who doesn't think like them."

"But Siamak doesn't hate anybody. You must have seen that. He loves people."

"Which people? I couldn't recognize or touch the working class he portrayed for me. He saw workers as things, not human beings. Siamak is like the rest of us, he's fascinated by himself and his ideas. He can't see anybody except himself, anything but his goal. His goal, in my opinion, is an illusion, invented in his own mind."

She became quiet for a while, as if she wanted to collect her strength. "You know Ramin, if we continue these discussions, they will never end. I accept you as you are with your beliefs or without. As you say, I'm a landowner, and generation after generation I've been against your working class. You two, you might agree that neither of you are part of the proletariat. You just imagine yourself a supporter of the working class. Anyway, I am what I am. You know better than me who you are."

"I wish I knew what I am and where I belong. I like you, you're at least truthful about yourself and don't deny your class. But I still don't know which class I belong to."

"It's not necessary to be tied to the tail of a class. Without that connection you can still be a human being."

"Only idealists think like that."

She stopped eating, reddened with rage, then swallowed her anger and said, "It's better we stop now."

"Why are you getting angry with me? I didn't say anything to hurt you. For me, responsibility is the most important thing. That is what I've learned from Siamak."

"But I'm not responsible for what happened between him and me. What Siamak did wasn't my responsibility. It was his."

"It depends on how you look at it."

She pushed aside her plate with food still on it; a smothered rage made her words hoarse. "Perhaps you expected me to offer myself to him."

Ramin said nothing. He too, set aside his half-eaten plate. The coldness in his eyes killed the words in Afsaneh.

They drove through dark, empty streets. Their meeting was not just disturbed by Siamak, it had become hostile. Afsaneh was angry with Siamak, with Ramin, and with herself as well. She had a vague sense she had missed out on Ramin in this game. She didn't know what to do to regain their intimacy. Ramin was silent, and she didn't want to — she couldn't — break the silence. She needed to think. She didn't picture herself as guilty. Ramin considered her at fault and she was annoyed. She had expected Ramin to understand her and now she didn't understand him. They were near Ramin's house and would have to separate. It wasn't clear when they could see each other again. Afsaneh spoke.

"Yes, it was my fault. If I'd slept with him, I would have spent those few days happily; Siamak, too. And now you wouldn't be sulking. Then I could have credit among your friends and fellow-thinkers as Siamak's lover."

She wanted to say, you might give me credit, too, but she didn't. She smothered her anger and tears, without finishing her words. Ramin looked at her in the dim light. Her scarf had fallen from her head and her curly hair looked like a hat.

He said, "We agreed not to talk about it again. Whatever happened, it's over now. Siamak isn't here to defend himself. Judge him as you like. But for me, just one thing is important: to take responsibility on our shoulders for whatever we make happen. This is what I've learned from Siamak."

They reached Ramin's house. Afsaneh put on the brake, looked at Ramin, and said, "What do you mean? What is my responsibility in this?"

"It's better I get out quickly," Ramin said, "these days everywhere is full of…"

He opened the car door. Afsaneh didn't expect him to leave her without answering.

"We'll talk about it later," he said. "Just remember that human responsibility is very important."

Firoozeh drank her tea and put the empty cup on the saucer. Her chador had fallen from her head and her fair, wavy hair poured onto her shoulders. Some gray hairs showed, but according to what Ozra had said, she would only be thirty-two or thirty-three. She looked older, wrinkles were visible in her fair complexion under her eyes. Her cheeks were red and fat, her large lips unlike Ozra's narrow lips and small mouth. She looked like the few pale photographs of the grandmother Afsaneh vaguely remembered. She didn't resemble Afsaneh's father at all. Nor had Majid Khan left any trace on Firoozeh's face. Afsaneh asked herself, who is her father?

"My dear Khanum. Today I've come here to talk to you. If you knew how Asad is behaving toward me! Since he found out I'm an illegitimate child, he abuses me to death. I can't take it any more. I can't live with this shame. Do you think I had a happy life in his uncle's house? I haven't talked about my life to anybody. How can I talk about it? It's a disgrace, it's a shame. If you knew how much I suffered. Khanum, why didn't my mother suffocate me? Why didn't she throw me in a sewer? God knows I would be released from this hard life. Do you think I had an ordinary life? That bastard father. Not a father, if he was a father, he wouldn't have tortured me. How can I explain it to you? It's not easy to talk about these things. I've had them with me all my life. I've kept them in my heart. They're like a lump in me, a knot, ready to strangle me. I have to talk to someone. Who better than you? The first day I met you, I liked your honesty, your generosity. I told myself, even if you weren't really my sister, and you accepted me in your house, it would be like I found a sister. I have nobody, never had a family. I've not seen my mother. What was she like? I wished I'd seen her for a moment. I wish she hadn't given me to this family. This family! What can I say about them? Not a family, they were wolves, male and female wolves. Sucking my blood. That bastard stepfather, when I remember how he made me suffer, I tremble with fear and shame."

She stared at Afsaneh, her eyes full of tears, and became quiet. Afsaneh couldn't believe what she was saying. She offered cookies to Firoozeh. She took one and put it on a plate close to herself.

"I was twelve when he came to me one night. From twelve to sixteen, when I married Asad, he came to me sometimes, covered my mouth and did something to me that a dog won't do to another dog. I didn't dare say anything. One day, my stepmother saw him put his hand under my skirt. Khanum, you can't imagine how she tormented me. If I had died it would have been better. She checked I hadn't lost my virginity, then she hit me and said, 'It was your fault.' I stayed quiet. It was a sin. How could I talk about it? They made me feel like a dog."

Minutes passed in silence. Firoozeh's eyes stared at Afsaneh brimming with tears and sadness. She continued, "Khanum, I should have died. Ozra should have drowned me in the water. After I was Asad's wife, do you think my torture was over? No, I swear to God, I didn't dare say anything to Asad. He's like a hungry wolf, cruel. He wants me to bear him a son. If this one is a girl, what can I do? Since he learned I was an illegitimate child, I'm like a tiny, unimportant pebble. He curses me in front of my children. Khanum, I have three daughters. You've seen my girls. I took care of them like flowers. I'm educated to grade eight. I want my daughters to study and be educated. All these miseries come from illiteracy. If Asad were educated, he wouldn't curse me in front of my children. My eldest daughter, Manijeh, she is withering away. She's not a child anymore, she is thirteen. She understands everything. Two years ago, he was on the side of the Shah and the white revolution. He chose his daughter's names from our *Shahnameh*. Now he has become a member of Hezbolah, and supports Imam Khomeini and Imam Hussein. I wish Imam

Hussein would strike him dead. He has ruined my children's lives and mine. Khanum, accept me as your maid, me and my three children."

She hit her belly with her fist and continued, "This one? I didn't want to have more children. What can a boy do for me? He will probably turn out like Asad. I don't want that. If I had a place, to rescue those three. What's the use of this sort of life? I don't want to go on living. I wish Ozra had thrown me in a sewer. I wish she'd smothered me. Is this a life?"

Afsaneh shook herself and sat up in her sleeping bag. She heard footsteps outside the tent. Darkness covered her like a sea covering all the creatures in it. She had forgotten where she was. The night and the darkness surrounded her, took her away. Ramin was lost to her. She hugged her knees and listened to the voices outside. The silence was like rubble falling on her and the world around her. She would be lonely forever. She yearned to join the silence.

Manijeh sobbed on the phone.

"Khanum, help us. My mother killed herself. She drank a bowl of poison and killed herself. Today she took Ameneh to the bath. Katayoon, Soodabeh and I were with her too. I helped her bathe Katayoon and Soodabeh and sent them out. Then I went home, and brought Ameneh. She washed her too and gave her to me. I took Ameneh home, then someone came from the *hamam* and informed us that my mother..."

Manijeh didn't continue. The phone disconnected. Afsaneh left the house. When she got there, the coroner had confirmed the suicide. Asad moved close to her, crying. She turned away from him and didn't stay. She couldn't stay. She didn't attend Firoozeh's burial or her memorial, either. She couldn't bear it. She went to the north and spent five days in Majid Khan's villa. She sat by the window and hugged her knees, watching the turbulent sea. It rained every day. She returned home with another knot tied in her heart, and went back to her normal life.

"Khanum, I don't deserve to be your sister. Don't believe Asad's words. You're like an angel. Believe me, you're an angel and you're not aware of it."

Afsaneh had gone to Firoozeh's home with her hands full — something for Manijeh, Katayoon and Soudabeh. The girls surrounded her. Soudabeh was five years old. She had something of Ozra in her. She was the only one who had Ozra's and Firoozeh's green eyes. The two others looked more like Asad. Manijeh had Firoozeh's gentleness. Her eyes were full of words, spoken in silence. At thirteen, she looked like a mature woman. When they moved to the Iran Street apartment, they seemed to spread their wings. The apartment became full of life and joy. Before, confined in those two rooms, they were like plants without sufficient water or light. They pressed against each other and withered. There was always quarreling among them. They were in their mother's way and made her nervous. But they bloomed in the spacious apartment, talkative and full of laughter. Whenever she went to visit them, Afsaneh noticed their blossoming. When Asad wasn't there, they showed more joy and were noisier. In Asad's presence they became timid. The change in behavior was most obvious in Manijeh. Firoozeh was outwardly quiet and calm. Her silence was annoying. She thanked Afsaneh in different ways, and then became quiet. Her belly was getting bigger.

Firoozeh didn't talk about her bitter memories. Sometimes she made things difficult for Afsaneh, too. When Afsaneh didn't visit, Firoozeh sent Manijeh to call from a public telephone and ask her why. Afsaneh didn't know what to do with this sister, this cousin, this stranger. She couldn't fit in with them or leave them alone and not think about them. They were an obligation she had inherited. She had lost Ramin, and found Firoozeh and her children.

Sometimes she told herself, if it hadn't happened like this, what would I do? She was so busy with Firoozeh and her children that she forgot about Ramin. Ramin slowly became a memory. Fridays she went hiking alone. Memories were everywhere. Fridays she talked to him, about Firoozeh, about Ozra, and about the children. She tearfully retold Firoozeh's life. She wiped the tears from her eyes, smiled and called herself crazy. In the afternoon, she returned home, tired and sad. Her apartment looked emptier and the words stayed with her, rotting away inside. She went to see Firoozeh, and if Asad was there, she regretted her visit. Asad would humiliate Firoozeh and the children in front of her. She decided to encourage Firoozeh to separate from Asad. When Afsaneh mentioned it to Firoozeh, she said, "How can I Khanum? I can't even think about it. He wants to go to court, to claim my father's wealth. My father? Who was my father? I don't know who my father was, and he wants to claim his wealth."

Afsaneh couldn't tolerate Asad. She had to leave. Night spread across the city. She wished she could go to the restaurant on Shemiran Road. But she didn't. She didn't like to go by herself and sit there while eyes watched her. Instead she drove her Renault through the empty streets of the upper section of the city, and everywhere Ramin was with her.

"I want to see you. Where are you these days? I know it's because of Siamak but it wasn't my fault, believe me. I can't …"

"It's not because of him. We have to be cautious. I don't stay at my own house, either. I might be forced to leave Iran."

"What do you mean?"

"It's hard to explain. When I see you, I'll tell you."

"When can we meet?"

She wanted to say, I have to tell you something important; she didn't. Did he love Negar? Those last days, what did he want to say? It wasn't her fault Negar was vulnerable and sensitive.

She didn't hear from him for two weeks. She called his home several times, but he wasn't there. One early winter evening, she didn't even light a candle. The power was out again. She didn't sit by the window, either. She just listened for the telephone to ring, and when it rang, her heart beat faster. When it wasn't him; she was immobilized. Crumpling on a sofa, she fell asleep. When she woke up, the electricity was back and all her lamps were on. She didn't even want to go to her bedroom or sleep in her own bed.

It was the middle of winter. The cloudy sky warned of snow. For three days Afsaneh hadn't left home. She felt desperate. Majid Khan had called her from France the night before and told her if the universities were still closed, she would do better to go to France and finish her education. She answered that because she had only a few courses left, she would prefer to stay here. Then she thought, she could talk about it with Ramin and go to France with him.

She jumped up at the sound of the doorbell. Before listening to the intercom, she opened the window. A wave of cold air rushed in. Afsaneh stretched her head out and saw Ramin with a woman wearing a black chador. She opened the apartment door, asking herself, who could that be?

She was shocked to see Negar with Ramin. Negar came in and took the chador off, combing her hair with her fingers. The conversation didn't flow. There was something between them. They had married. They talked about fleeing across the border. Fleeing across the border with a smuggler, saying goodbye. And then she realized they'd been married for a week. She froze. She wanted to talk about leaving for France, talk about her uncle who could send an invitation for Ramin, and pay for his education. Then she understood. She had lost Ramin. She grew cold. She didn't remember what she said after that. Her silence transmitted itself to Ramin, and he became quiet too. Only Negar chatted.

A lump rose in her throat, she rushed to the kitchen and smothered the tears. When they went to say goodbye, Ramin hugged her, and she was a stone. She kissed his cheeks, feeling his unshaved beard. Negar hugged her warmly and talked loudly. She said, "Pray for us to cross the border safely and not be captured by the guards." Afsaneh didn't ask which border they were crossing.

Ramin wanted to see her again. She refused and traveled to the North, to Majid Khan's villa, sat by the window and watched the sea. Coming back to Tehran, all the way back, she told herself, Ramin is dead.

Six years later when she met Bahram, she saw a touch of Ramin in him, for a second. A few months later, dining in a restaurant, Bahram asked her to marry him and she accepted. She invited Bahram to her place the same night, and slept with him, looking in vain for Ramin in him. She lived with Bahram for two years and five months, expecting to have children. But it didn't happen. When she met Ramin in a Montreal Street with Negar and Damon, she still didn't know about Bahram's sterilization. Again she told herself, Ramin is dead. He's another man, he has a wife and child.

A year and half later she was in a Toronto restaurant, near Yonge and Eglinton, dining with Eliot. Eliot had asked her several times to dine with him, or have a coffee, but she had refused. She felt Eliot looking at her in a way different from the way a principal looks at a childcare assistant. When he met her in the office or in the hallways, he stared at her, and when he talked to her, he didn't take his eyes off her. One Friday, Afsaneh was arranging the classroom for Monday morning. Nadia had left early to take her child to a doctor. Afsaneh was picking up scrap paper from the floor and tidying up the toys. Eliot was standing by the classroom door. She stood up, and saw him with a smile on his face.

"You work very hard. I appreciate it."

She said nothing. She didn't say that Nadia had to leave early. Nadia had probably informed the office.

Eliot walked closer. He looked directly into her eyes with the same desire he always had.

"Won't you accept my invitation for once?"

It was Friday night and she had nothing to do. She didn't want to go to Ramin's place. She had decided to see them less and not be hurt by Negar's indifference.

Afsaneh smiled. Eliot accepted her smile as a good sign and said, "What about tonight?"

She nodded confirmation.

That night, Eliot talked about his life. His wife had left him five years ago, had taken away his ten and six-year-old daughters.

"And you can't see them?"

"I could, until a few months ago. They stayed two nights with me every two weeks. But then my wife moved to California to live with her boyfriend."

"And you couldn't get the children from her?"

"No, she has custody of the children. Even if I could, I wouldn't do it. She loves the children."

Eliot asked her to marry him a month later. He said he always admired Eastern women, he had heard about their dignity and sincerity. He talked about their age difference saying he realized fifty-two was a little late for marriage, but when there is understanding and love, differences vanish.

Afsaneh agreed with him and said, yes, when there is love and understanding... She didn't say she had no love for him. After that she tried not to be where he was. When she saw him, she pretended she didn't. Two weeks after school closed for summer holidays, Eliot called her home and again proposed marriage. "I know I'm older than you," he said, "but I can make you happy." He talked about his big suburban house, his cottage on the shore of Georgian Bay, and about his parents, wealthy farmers with a large farm in northern Ontario. Afsaneh listened to him in silence. He said, "I love you. Don't think that I want to buy you. I just wanted you to know more about me. Something in you has captivated me. You're like your storyteller, Sheharazade. I associate your name with stories too." Afsaneh still listened to him quietly. He said, "You are like a closed book."

She repeated, "A closed book!" Then she remained quiet.

Eliot asked her, "Why don't you say anything?"

Afsaneh explained briefly that she hadn't thought about marrying again. Eliot suggested he would be just a friend, that they could see each other sometimes, get to know each other better.

"No," Afsaneh answered.

Surprised, Eliot said, "What kind of person are you? I would like to know you better."

Afsaneh repeated loudly, "Me, me? Who am I? And what do I want? What am I doing here? I can't stay here forever."

Her mind cleared. She thought about tomorrow. Tomorrow she should go back to the city, start life again, have a friendship with Ramin and Negar, endure Negar, love Ramin from a distance, sleep in a lonely bed, denied Ramin's love, grasp the sheet with anger to smother her cries and witness the passing of life till she was old.

"No." Afsaneh screamed, and left the tent. A light glimmered among the trees. There were people in the campground. The weather was cold and the moon was a sparkling circle in the sky, spreading light. She put on warm clothes, walked through the trees to the lake. The moon seemed bigger over the lake. The surface of the lake was calm and the moonlight reflected in small waves, turning them silvery.

The moon shone into the depths of the pond as if the pond was as far away as the sky, a mysterious world with another moon, which frightened, fascinated and charmed Afsaneh. Ozra held her hand to take her to her room. But Afsaneh fought to stay and watch the moon in the sky and at the bottom of the pond, trembling in the water, then round, shiny and full again as if it was two moons, one high in the sky and the other at the bottom of the black pond water.

"Let's go, girl, the pond mother will drag you to the bottom."

"Where's the pond mother? Why don't I see her?"

"The pond mother? Nobody sees the pond mother. If you saw her, her bewitching power would disappear. The pond mother is the mother of all genies."

"Ozra, show me the genies, where are they?"

Ozra said, "Call on God. The genies are hidden somewhere. Look into the pond, they are all there. If I say something to hurt them, they'll grab our legs and drag both of us into the pond. The pond mother sits at the bottom of the pond and drags all bad children into the water to drown them. Let's go make dinner."

Afsaneh didn't want to leave the pond. She wanted to see the pond mother and the genies. There were genies in the yard. She looked for them in the trembling shadow of the lantern on the walls and the trellis of vine leaves. Through Ozra she believed in the genies' existence. Sometimes Afsaneh imagined she had seen them, like shadows, running in front of her or following her. When she turned to see them, they disappeared. Ozra said to ask God to make the genies disappear. Afsaneh asked God but she loved genies. As Ozra said, genies were always happy - dancing and singing. Nights when Samad Khan and Sara went horseback riding, Afsaneh sat on Ozra's lap and Ozra told her tales about genies. She dreamed about them in her sleep, imagined seeing them.

Genies were dancing on the surface of the lake, running everywhere with the breeze.

"Have you seen genies?"

"Me? Genies? Why do you think about genies?"

"When I was a child, my playmates were genies."

She was startled by Ramin's loud laugh. "Are you joking?"

"I'm not joking. I heard so much about them, I believed I knew them. I called them by name."

"For you, that seems strange. You who are so fearless that you go to the sea to swim at night."

"What's the problem with night? Everybody thinks the sea at night is frightening, but it's not. A sea is the same, day or night. I don't like the flush of the day, everything is so ordinary. Day is like a burden on human shoulders. Day is work. There's always something to do. Responsibilities, studying, working, visit this one and that one, clean the house, cook, shop, eat, bathe, thousands of chores, small and large. Sometimes I think most of these chores are just wasting time, killing time. But at night, everybody is free. You spend time as you like. You read, watch TV, watch a film, sit and listen to the silence, carried by the passing of time leading to death.

"Death? Do you think about death, too?"

"Death flows in my veins. How can I not think about death? I try not to think about death, I try to think about life, about the moment. I like the here and now, especially this night full of secrets. I would like to know it, to be absorbed by it. Nights have a strange magic, a magic which puts all creatures to sleep."

Afsaneh forced Ramin to follow her into the lake, where the water reached their necks. Standing, she took Ramin's face in her hands, "If you knew how difficult the years away from you were!"

Ramin said nothing. She wanted to pull words out of him, like the first night when she wanted him to tell her, we'll be together forever. She put his head on her shoulder and said, "I'm tired, dead tired, save me, protect me, I need you." Caressing his hair, her slender fingers travelled over his body.

"It can be over. From now on we can be together, just me and you."

The first night they didn't sleep at all. They discovered themselves and their bodies like travellers arriving in a fascinating land. In the morning, elated, half awake, they went for food and wood.

That afternoon and evening they spent in the lake, as if their souls and bodies needed to be cleansed. They didn't talk about the past or their future, it was as if they didn't exist. They were two strange voyagers, meeting. Hand in hand they embraced, expressing their love with long kisses. Moments later, they were inflamed. Into the tent, where they wove into each other like two trees with the same root. They didn't sit and talk about what had happened, about Damon and Negar, and decide what to do. Time existed only in the moments spent together.

It was Ramin who said, "Is it possible to keep this moment as it is, as we are, in each others arms, and change into a stone, die, disappear, evaporate and fly up to the sky?"

"But I prefer to be alive, to feel these trees, this water, this night."

"He didn't change into a stone. He left me. He preferred his hateful life to death. He preferred that life to me. He went to die slowly, little by little. He went to be sacrificed. He didn't want to be with me. I would give him life, I would give him love, I was ready..."

Afsaneh was sitting on a rock by the lake. A cold breeze blew. She trembled. Her head on her knees, tears washed her face. Voices drifted in from far away. She lifted her head and saw shadows, and a trembling light, moving. Voices in the wind.

"I can't believe that a moment of negligence, a sentence, a word can ruin a person's entire life. Sometimes I think I was sacrificed by my own negligence. I sacrificed my dreams because I didn't believe them. I just wanted to know the world. The dreams my father planted in me, they weren't ever clear to me. I didn't know how to make them real. When I was a child, my father always talked about an ideal society. He was a pessimist, but he had dreams which he talked about to us. He talked about a society with social justice and equal access to everything for everybody. I didn't understand what social justice meant. To tell the truth, I don't understand it now, either. I never did. The questions are getting more complicated for me. Now I'm bewildered. You see that I've lost my power to act. I believe anything. You see how futile and useless I've become!"

"It's not your fault. The situation became impossible. When the wall of faith collapsed..."

"Faith? What faith? I didn't have faith. Whatever my father planted in me, didn't grow, didn't take root. I didn't know my own self. I couldn't be truthful to myself. When I met you, I was pulled towards you with all my being, but I didn't believe my feelings. I denied my feelings. I was confused. I was still a fourteen-year-old boy formed by my father, full of my father's memories, full of heroic stories, of defeats, executions, poems, *Shahnameh's* myths. I wanted to be *Siavoush, Rostam, Sohrab.* I wanted to be pure, I wanted to be a hero."

"Did my love...?"

"No, no, it wasn't you. It was me who imagined love as a sin. Love in that atmosphere was a sin. Love in that situation! Do you remember?"

"And now that..."

"There's no now. I've lost my life. I wanted to play hero and it didn't work. I couldn't do it."

"You just chose the wrong way. You didn't lose."

"I chose the only way that was in front of me. I had to choose that way, if I wanted to be a hero. And I lost. I lost my life."

"But you're still alive, you're still young."

"Alive? Do you call this life? This exile? This rootlessness? This ordeal?"

"Exile isn't a new thing. You can get used to it. Complaining won't solve the problem."

"Yes, but it's too late."

"Now that you know, you can go back. Any mistake is retrievable. As they say 'every fish pulled from the sea is fresh.' You have the right to live as you like."

"Yes, but it's too late. Perhaps four or five years ago, before Damon was born, I could go my way, but now with another one on the way, how can I?"

"Everybody is always sorry for his or her own past, but it's never too late to start again."

"To start what?"

"To start your life."

"I've lost my life."

"But you're still alive."

"I'm not. Half of me is buried in the past in Iran and half buried here in the present."

"Buried with Siamak."

"You may not believe it, or you may think I'm making too much of it, but you're right. Half of me was buried with Siamak and the other Siamaks. I always tell myself, what was the difference between them and me? Their only fault was that they were captured, and our luck was that we could flee."

"You can be the continuation of the lost Siamak."

"I wish I could."

"If you want to, you can. If you didn't worship death so much, you could. You're like a person standing on top of a high wall, scared to move. You should think about coming down from the wall. There must be a way. You can't think about a solution when you are standing, shaking, on top of a wall. My dear, life doesn't repeat itself."

"And it's not important how you spend it. You have to enjoy it. Is that what you want to say?"

"No, I don't want to say that. I want to say that you should sacrifice yourself . You should stay on the top of that wall until you die of fear or old age, while below, life goes on, life thrives."

"Yes, you always overwhelmed me with your words, but you know that behind these words there's nothing but illusion. Why don't you enjoy your life? Why don't you enjoy life's possibilities?"

"I lost my love. I found my love among those who want to sacrifice themselves."

"So you were sacrificed in some way as well."

"Sacrificed to you."

Breezes blew through the trees, leaves rattled. The moon shone on the surface of the lake — big and bright, glowing like a silver tray — sliding to the west. A few stars glimmered. Afsaneh only paid attention to the moon. As if there was just the moon and herself, and everything that passed through her mind was no secret to the moon. The small waves reflected the moon's silvery light. Last night they had been in the lake until late. Hanging from Ramin's neck, she shared her happiness with the moon. But tonight the moon was sad and worried.

A cold wind blew through her clothes, penetrated her skin and bones. Afsaneh shivered. It wasn't just the cold wind which made her shiver, she felt the chill inside. Everything seemed murky. The moon was hidden behind the trees, flitted among branches shaking with the wind. The moon and the lake weren't clear any more. Only darkness and silence. The presence of death, death in the lake, death at night, death among the trees, surrounded her. Death was in her breath, her bones, her veins. Death wasn't under the soil, but above it. Alive and breathing.

Afsaneh walked over the gravestones. The night before, she had dreamed of Ozra, and Firoozeh. Sometimes it was Ozra and sometimes Firoozeh. She woke in the middle of the night and only slowly fell back to sleep. This time, she dreamed of Ozra. They were in the house in Sarcheshmeh, and then the house in Varamin. Ozra was sitting by the pond. Afsaneh wasn't a child, but an adult, and sad. Ozra was hard on her. She said to Ozra, "It wasn't just you who suffered because of Hoorie's absence, I did too."

She didn't want to admit she was in love, even to herself. She wanted to forget him.

Ozra scolded her, "Why didn't you do something? Why did you let her kill herself?"

"What could I do? He married his cousin. He wanted to rescue her and himself."

"I'm talking about Hoorie."

"Not Hoorie, Firoozeh," she said, "I saw her, Ozra. I saw your Hoorie. She had green eyes like you thought."

"And you let her eat a bowl of poison and my four grandchildren become motherless. You're like your mother, thinking only about your own love."

She saw Ozra, sitting by the pond, scolding her with her staring eyes, making ripples in the water. There were waves on the pond. Ozra was talking, but didn't look at Afsaneh.

"You were right Ozra, Hoorie had green eyes," Afsaneh said.

She woke up. Ozra wasn't there any more. It was morning. Afsaneh was wet with the sweat of the summer heat. Getting up, she went to the kitchen, took a bottle of water from the fridge and drank. It was a hot day. The electricity was off. Stifling heat, and Ozra's presence wouldn't leave her alone. In the afternoon, when slanting sunshine lengthened the shadows, Afsaneh put on a black dress with a black scarf, took her black chador and left the house for Beheshte Zahra cemetery. She bought flowers and rosewater on the way to the cemetery. She knew where the grave was; Asad had called her the day after Firoozeh's burial to tell her. She wrote it down in a notebook by the telephone, but she didn't go.

Beheshte Zahra was full of crowds. She remembered it was Thursday afternoon and many mourners were there to be with their deceased. She passed among veiled women, unshaven men and new graves. Her eyes read the stones, looking for Firoozeh. She was surprised to see gravestones for so many students and teenagers. The university and high school classes had gone underground. When she read the name Siamak Selahi on a grave, she stopped walking, shocked. A man the same height as Siamak with gray hair and a few days unshaven beard was watering a pot of geraniums with a green plastic pitcher. He watered the plant carefully, as if afraid to hurt the red geraniums. Then he poured the rest of the water on the gravestone. A woman in a black chador was sitting by the grave, her chador pulled down over her face. Afsaneh looked at the man and saw traces of Siamak in him. Her hands and her feet went cold. She read the script on the gravestone, date of birth, date of death. Obviously, it was Siamak. Sitting by the grave for awhile she pretended to be reading verses for the dead. She put the flowers on the grave and emptied the bottle of rosewater on it, listening to the beating of her own heart. His date of death was after Ramin's departure. The woman lifted her head, pulled aside her chador and looked at Afsaneh, surprised. Afsaneh got up, saying goodbye quietly and left. She couldn't introduce herself.

A few graves further on, she found Firoozeh. Afsaneh didn't have anymore flowers or rosewater. She looked around for a flower peddler, but didn't see one. She said, "Next time, when I come to your grave, I'll bring a big bouquet of flowers."

But she knew she wouldn't come. She didn't feel death under the gravestones. Death was with her. Firoozeh wasn't under that stone, but buried under life's pains. Only her body was under that soil. Her memories were with Afsaneh, memories filled with painful words.

Afsaneh sat by the grave for a few minutes. Inside a voice was talking to her about the uselessness of this visit. She knew she did it for Ozra, but because she had nothing to offer Firoozeh's grave, she heard Ozra scolding her again. Getting up, she decided to go back to the entrance area to buy flowers and rosewater. She passed Siamak's grave again. This time she didn't see his father and mother. The pot of geraniums was broken, the plant crushed and strewn. A few young men were walking away singing slogans. When she got into her Renault to go for flowers, she doubted she'd come back. "Forgive me Firoozeh. What difference does it make to you that flowers cover your grave? Nobody knew you. You're not a martyr with a crown of honour on your head. You committed suicide. You chose the most painful death. You turned your back on life. You were brave, but no one admired your courage."

Afsaneh's eyes were burning, but she had no tears. Her bones shivered with the cold. She remembered Firoozeh's daughters. She had seen Manijeh several times, hiking with a young man. Manijeh said she had been accepted by the university and had become engaged. Both of them were studying engineering in Sharif University. Manijeh was studying chemical engineering, and the boy, what was his name? Afsaneh had forgotten what he was studying? Manijeh had told her he was in his last year of university. Manijeh invited her to the wedding, but she didn't go. It was when she was going to Canada.

Sussan, Bahram's cousin, told her Bahram had a child with an Arab woman in Canada and that his father didn't let him marry her. Bahram left Iran for Canada suddenly, because of a big bribery scandal in his company. Bahram's close friend, Mahmood, who worked in the same company, had called Bahram, and a few days later Bahram left Iran without giving Afsaneh a clear explanation. He briefly told her he had to leave because of urgent work in Montreal. And that he was afraid he might be considered a suspect. He left within a week, without waiting for Afsaneh to go with him. She was waiting for her immigration papers, and in the interval sometimes wondered whether she should follow Bahram or not. She wasn't sure about having children with him. When Sussan told her about Bahram's illegitimate child, she thought she might have a problem. Afsaneh decided to go and see a gynecologist in Canada. She was reluctant to immigrate to Canada because she had heard Ramin and Negar were there. When she finally decided to go, she rented her apartment to Manijeh with a promise that if she returned, they would give it back to her.

That summer afternoon, in downtown Montreal, when she met Ramin carrying his two-year-old son on his shoulders, her heart sank. No one, not even Negar, who was a cunning woman, discovered how disturbed she was. At night beside Bahram in their bed, she was like a piece of stone. Afsaneh even briefly lost her desire to have a baby.

At first, neither Ramin nor Negar recognized her. Negar, at twenty-four, had lost her teenage features and become a slender young woman with blond hair and a made-up face. She wore a sleeveless, open-collared blouse, her skin tanned in places. Her eyes, hair gave her a European look. Ramin's complexion was paler, too. There was gray hair sprinkled amongst the black, and tiny wrinkles around his eyes. He had a tired face, in spite of his smile.

After a bit Negar recognized her. They were all astounded and for awhile couldn't speak.

Negar started to talk first, saying Afsaneh had changed, become younger and prettier. She said it was because of the beautiful country of Canada, and called it their homeland.

Afsaneh invited them to an ice cream parlour close by and all the while amused Damon, who was shy with her in the beginning, and didn't want to sit on her lap. And then he didn't want to leave her lap. She said, "Give him to me, and have another child for yourself."

"Don't you have any?" asked Negar.

She sighed and said, "Not yet."

Negar asked again, "Why not? After two years, it's time to have babies."

Ramin stared at her in silence. Their eyes met sometimes. There was a wondering look in Ramin's eyes. He looked wiser, as if busy with his own thoughts. She couldn't tell whether Ramin was happy to see her or not.

That night she was quiet. She dined with Bahram in a restaurant, ignoring his jokes. When they came home, she sat on the balcony, facing the St. Lawrence River, and watched the city, lit by thousands of lamps.

Afsaneh didn't mention Ramin to Bahram, and as her life continued with Bahram, she felt a distance grow between them. She wondered why she wanted to have children with a man she didn't love. She became more and more quiet. The memories she had of Ramin and their short time were revived. Sometimes she imagined herself in Negar's place and rejoiced. Bahram, meanwhile, was a stranger to her soul. He didn't understand what was going on. He ignored her desire to have children. He just wanted to enjoy his time with her. To be happy and enjoy life was his only aim. Dining in different restaurants and tasting expensive wines, or spending time in bars had been interesting for Afsaneh at the beginning, but she quickly tired of it. She couldn't find what she was looking for in this country either. Her home was empty, her heart was empty. When she decided to say what she felt to Bahram, she didn't imagine it leading to separation. Bahram revealed his past to her, and sobbed. She felt pity for him, in spite of the hate burning in her. His hands on her body made her shudder. Out of pity, she promised to stay with him and then regretted it. Why? For whom? She asked him to adopt a child and told him she'd go to Iran and bring back a child. Bahram wouldn't agree.

"I can't. Do you think I sterilized myself for no reason? I can't have children. Every child reminds me of Hanna's girl, my own girl, a girl I lost."

Bahram got drunk. Whenever Afsaneh talked about a child, he became angry. When he was at home, she hid herself in the library pretending to read. She ignored him and didn't answer his questions. She was careless with the housework. One night their quarrel became vicious. She took refuge in the library and locked the door. Bahram forced the door open, lifted her from the couch and tore her dress, wanting to have sex. She kicked him with an anger that was unusual for her and left.

Afsaneh remembered that cold night painfully; wind lifted snow from roofs and sidewalks, blew it on passing faces. She spent the night at a friend's place and the next morning left Montreal for Toronto, never to return. Her life with Bahram was a closed book, she didn't want to look at or talk about. Not with Negar who asked about it, nor with others. She talked to Ramin these last few nights. Whenever Ramin spoke about his painful past, she showed him a few pages from her own book, to let him know that she had wasted her life as well.

Afsaneh walked along the beach. Coldness penetrated her bones, she shivered. She didn't think about warming herself. She yielded to the cold. She walked and looked at the ground. The lake was motionless. The moon shone among the foliage. Her eyes became accustomed to the darkness and she could see the ground beneath her feet. Pebbles covered the beach. She bent and took a pebble, felt its weight in her hand. Holding the pebble in her hand, she studied it.

"I wish I could change to a stone this very moment."

She envied the stone. The mystery in its coldness and silence. She asked herself, what about me? Can I be a stone? She stopped walking, trembling. A feeling of alienation took hold and she asked herself, "What am I doing here?"

Again she envied the stone. She wanted to be a stone. If she was a stone, she would have a place. Now, she didn't know where she should be. Where? She had no place to be. No place to spend the night, tomorrow or beyond. She bent again, took a handful of pebbles and stuffed them in her pockets. The coldness had left her, but she was anxious. The stones gave her confidence. She felt the weight of being and belonging somewhere. She filled her pockets with more pebbles.

She heard a rattling among the trees, and listened, "What if it's a bear?" She smiled as a raccoon brushed past her.

Afsaneh walked into the water. It was warmer than the air.

Into the water without a clear thought, into the water, as she did every night. The water gave her refuge. She felt Ramin beside her. When the water reached her neck, she stopped, and put her head under the water. She heard Ramin's voice. She looked up at the beach and didn't see anybody. She saw the pale outline of trees far away. On the north side, among the trees, was a light, a cottage perhaps, with windows lit. A light moved toward her on the lake, then turned and sailed away. She plunged her head under the water again, and heard Ramin's voice, calling her name. Afsaneh brought her head out of water and looked around. There was no movement. She stretched out in the water for a moment, plunged in slowly, and heard Ramin's voice, indistinct and far away, calling her. Perhaps he's at the bottom of the lake," she thought.

"Accept that I can't. Believe me, I can't. What do I say to Negar? To Damon? I have responsibilities."

"Please, don't talk about responsibilities. Just tell me, do you love me or not?"

"Oh, again? You know better than me how much I love you. All these years there wasn't a single day I haven't thought about you but..."

"But what? We can leave this city. We'll take Damon with us. We can go somewhere where no one will know us, like this spot, under these trees."

"Don't be a child, Afsaneh."

"So, tell me you love me. Tell me you'll love me forever."

"What's the use of these conversations? You shouldn't sacrifice yourself for love."

He went away. She knew he would go. She knew it from the first moment they came together and revived their love. She was sure he would go.

She heard Ramin's voice indistinct and far away. Was it Ramin, calling her? Her mind was dull.

"Who's calling me? It's the pond mother calling me."

"Don't go near the pond. Look, the pond mother is at the bottom of the pond, she will drag you into the water."

"Ramin is calling me."

"It's not Ramin. It's the pond mother. The voice is coming from the bottom of the water. Genies, perhaps."

The voice echoed inside the water. A hand grabbed her, a body wove into hers. Ramin was with her.

She laughed loudly and wrapped Ramin in her arms.

"Let's go to the feast of the genies. Listen, the pond mother is calling me. Let's go."

Ramin struggled to pull her out. Afsaneh wrapped her arms around his neck.

"We'll be together for ever, for ever," Afsaneh whispered.

"If it's time to die, it would be better to die in the water. In the sea, or an ocean or even in this lake. The water would wash all the dirt from your body and soul. Without water there is death."

"You can die in water, too."

"Death in the water is beautiful. It's like making love to water for life. Death in water means making love with death and life at the same time. Isn't it beautiful, isn't it glorious?"

"Why do you talk so much about death?"

"I feel it. I always feel it. I smell its odour. I hear its voice. I was raised with death. Sara's death, Samad Khan's death, Ozra's death, Firoozeh's death. I've been living with these deaths. All those dead are living in me."

"Don't think about them."

"Is it possible not to? Why can't you stop thinking about Siamak?"

"Siamak didn't die. They killed him. He became a martyr and a martyr never dies. Did Hallaj die? Did Maziar and Babak die? They're part of our history."

"My dead are part of my history, too. They live in me, and as long I'm living, they live in me."

"So you admire death, too."

"No, I admire life, trees, the sky, stars, seas, water. I admire nature, the moon and soil, the soil which will embrace me one day, embrace me forever and let me be one with nature. Let me flow like sap in trees, in creeks to the ocean, change into mist and ascend to the sky, an element of cloud and rain, then penetrate into the earth and repeat the same cycle, the same cycle forever and ever. I want to take part in the cycle of nature."

❧ THREE ❧

The youth without memories greets you, asks you about his forgotten wish.

Pablo Neruda

SHE WAS GOING AN AGAIN about the wheat and lentil seeds which didn't sprout, how they rotted and she had to throw them out. I can't believe she's so superstitious, Ramin thought, why does she think it means something bad will happen? What could happen? Nothing will happen. Afsaneh isn't a silly woman. She knows how to manage. She's always managed, the failed sprouts are just superstition. Better not to think about it.

Ramin had left the camping area, walking quickly without looking back. The forest seemed quiet and content, golden light shining among the foliage, and birds singing occasionally. The afternoon silence was like a languid introduction to the cool, summer night, with the sun sent off the horizon. During his years in this country, summer had become a chance to go camping and drown in its overflowing greenness, an afternoon siesta in pleasant weather. When you wake up, the long night of winter with its mysterious solitude, is on the way.

Ramin walked on a narrow path among the trees. He heard a car noise behind him and was certain it was Afsaneh. He didn't look back. The car picked up speed and passed him.

"Accept it, Afsaneh. Don't be a child. This won't work for you and me."

Afsaneh wrapped her hands around his neck, kissing his face repeatedly, hanging onto him like bindweed.

"It is possible," she said, "this is life, not what you or I have. This is real life. Don't you believe in our love? Don't you? Don't tell me you don't believe in it."

"Afsaneh, there's no time left for love. It's too late. Why don't you want to understand?"

"No, it's not too late. It will never be too late, even if we live to be a hundred years old, it won't be too late. I've become young with you, I'm born again with you, and you..."

"But I have responsibilities."

"Our love doesn't affect your responsibilities."

"That's not so."

They were in a restaurant on Shemiran Street. The electricity was off. There was a small candle on every table. Close to the cash machine an oil lamp buzzed. Occasionally, the street was lit by car lights, then silence and darkness returned.

They were waiting for their dinner, less than two weeks after they had met. It was the third time they had dinner in a restaurant, each time at Afsaneh's invitation, which Ramin tried to turn down.

Afsaneh said, "Why don't you accept my invitation? Do you think you should pay? Don't worry about it. As you say, I'm a rich child of a landowner. I have money I don't know what to do with. I want to be a little lavish with my spending. Don't worry about my inheritance. I work and my income isn't bad. It's more than my expenses. I work at the French Institute and have private students, too. These days, everyone who can afford it wants to leave the country. Especially young people. With universities closed, they go somewhere else for education. If the government lets them.

"Even if you didn't work, you wouldn't be in need financially."

"I like to work. Working makes me feel alive. Gives me energy."

"Working and spending, bourgeois culture."

"I don't know any other."

He wanted to talk about poverty, about class separation and the unfair social system, but Afsaneh changed the subject.

"I don't disagree with you. What you say seems logical. But I don't have a solution. I have the right to enjoy my life."

"So you believe an individual's responsibility is to enjoy life."

"It depends on how you think about it."

Their conversations always reached an impasse. Afsaneh went quiet to end the discussion. Ramin was happy with Afsaneh, in spite of their different points of view. He felt as if he had known her for a long time, and when he said so, Afsaneh confirmed his feelings with an understanding smile of joy. He wanted to add, it may be because I don't have a sister. But Afsaneh wasn't a sister, or a friend. He never admitted that he loved her. No, she wasn't a lover.

"You seemed to have always existed in my life," Ramin said. "I always talked to someone in my head, the way I talk to you."

"You came out of the blue for me," Afsaneh said. "I never had someone to talk to, I mean, the way I talk to you. Well, everyone talks to many people, but not about everything."

The restaurant had to close earlier than other nights. A bomb alarm sent people hurriedly to their homes.

"Would you like to come to my place and have tea?" Afsaneh asked.

"No, my mother would be worried about me."

She gave him a ride home. He stood by his door until Afsaneh left, her Renault disappearing down the street.

Ramin arrived at the camp gate, which was freshly washed and waiting in the summer afternoon for newcomers from the city. A park employee was talking to a driver parked in front of an entrance building. Ignoring them, he walked out of the area. A car with a canoe on the roof and a shirtless driver passed him. Ramin walked faster, with no idea of the distance from the gate to the main highway. When he came to the park five days ago with Afsaneh, he was so disturbed and preoccupied, he paid no attention to how far they travelled. When he collected himself, Afsaneh was already erecting the tent. Ramin was still too confused to lift a finger to help Afsaneh. He left himself in her hands.

"I can't bear it any more. Believe me, I can't go on," he sobbed. After years, he had finally burst. Afsaneh moved closer to him hesitantly, then hugged him. He felt her take his face in her hands and lay his head on her chest. He could feel her warm body, hear her heart beating. He looked up. She stared into his eyes, wet with tears and compassion.

"What should I do? Tell me, what should I do?"

"What happened to make you torture yourself?"

"She's pregnant again."

"Pregnant? Well..."

"I can't afford it. I can't afford two. She never takes responsibility for anything. Tell me, what am I going to do? I can't bear it anymore." He sobbed again. The tears, in him for years, poured out and washed down his cheeks. Afsaneh held his face in her hands.

"Tell me what to do? I can't continue."

Their eyes fixed on each other. For how long, he didn't know. Afsaneh wrapped him in her arms, showered him with kisses repeating, "Let's go somewhere, somewhere far from here."

Walking along the road toward the main highway, Ramin was busy with his own thoughts. To his right was a grove of pine trees, scattered with dead trees, the greenness like skeletons. On his left was a vast stretch of land with a few high-rises sprouting from the earth, like warts on the land.

"It's better she didn't follow me. She has to understand, we can't go on. I couldn't go away with her. But what am I going to say to Negar? How do I face her? I won't say anything. It's not necessary, she knows everything. I'll tell her it was an emergency, I had to go out of the city. What kind of emergency? Why would I have emergency work? I won't talk to her at all. She must have found out. She knows I've left with Afsaneh. But I'll say nothing.

It's enough. If she wants to stay with me, she has to accept me. Accept me! If she doesn't, what is she going to do? Would she leave? To go where? Now she's pregnant. Why?"

He stopped walking. The road was like a crawling snake, its curves lost in the distance. The horizon was vast, the sun setting behind the trees. The road was covered in shade. He stood for a while. How long ago had he left the park? He didn't remember. His watch said it was after eight. He couldn't imagine how long he had been walking. When he left the camping area, shadows had began to fall and evening seemed close, but here, the horizon was vast. There was still daylight left.

"When I reach the main highway, I'll ask for a ride. And before nightfall I will be home."

He remembered Damon and smiled.

"I can't leave them. If you had children, you would understand me better."

"I love Damon as if he is my own child. You know how much I love him."

"But you don't have any responsibility for him."

"Love brings responsibilities, too."

"It's not just responsibilities. I have to stay. Damon won't forgive me."

"It's you who won't forgive yourself."

"You may be right. I have to go."

Tired, his legs numb, Ramin slowed down A car roared past him. He walked faster, hoping to reach the main highway but couldn't see any sign of it. A few hundred yards ahead of him trees lined both sides of the road. The path was darker and narrower.

They were in the lake. The moon was behind the trees flickering among the leaves and thousands of waves glimmered on the lake. Above was a cloudless sky, dark blue.

"Come on, don't be afraid."

Afsaneh held his hand and led him deep into the lake.

"I can't understand why people are afraid of water at night. Especially this lake, calm as a pool. Maybe you are afraid of the pond mother?"

"The pond mother?"

"Yes, Ozra always made me feel afraid of the pond mother. She used to say, the pond mother is the mother of all genies."

"And because of that you are so fearless?"

"What is there to be afraid of?"

"Death. I'm just afraid of death. I'm afraid something will happen to me, and I won't be able to..."

"Don't think about it. Death is always with us. I feel death with me, and I'm ready for it."

"You? I can't believe it. You are full of life. You're like a newly-opened blossom, since I met you again."

"From now on, our lives belong to us. Together. I can't believe it."

"I can't believe it, either. How did we live before this?"

"What about you?"

"I didn't have a life."

He pressed her to his chest. From her lips, he sucked the essence of all the nights and days when he was separated from her. They had been in the water since the moon rose over the lake. Afsaneh didn't want to get out.

"I wish I could sleep on the water, or even under the water."

"It's possible. You could find a way."

"Not in a boat or in a ship, right on the water."

Ramin reached the path through the trees. Day disappeared. He looked back. The last light was swallowed by evening. The first star signalled the coming night. He was afraid.

"What will she do tonight?"

He turned and looked back, expecting to see Afsaneh's car.

"She won't stay there. She wouldn't stay overnight in the campground."

He stopped walking. Night had descended abruptly, suddenly jumping out, as if it had been hiding among the trees. Even in the distance, the light had vanished, confirming night's invasion.

"I have to go back for her. I shouldn't leave her alone."

He turned around and walked a few steps. A car drove toward him. Its lights blocked his view. He stopped walking, hoping the car might be Afsaneh's. It roared by.

"Should I go back? No. If I do, she won't leave with me, and won't let me leave either. I know it. I have to keep going."

An hour after Afsaneh's phone call, Siamak knocked on his door and came in. Ramin guessed something had happened between he and Afsaneh. He couldn't believe Afsaneh had thrown him out. Ramin had woven a beautiful image of Afsaneh for Siamak. He wanted Siamak to know that even though she didn't believe in their ideas, even though she didn't consider herself one of them, there was much to admire in her. He had introduced her to Siamak as a reliable friend, and while Siamak was at her place Ramin felt happy. He was doing something valuable for Siamak. Siamak had captivated not only Ramin, but also many of his peers. His honesty and friendliness were adored. People were fascinated by him. When Siamak studied at the University of Tehran he made many friends, mostly girls who admired him. They asked for his telephone number and called him at home. Ramin heard about it and made jokes, asking Siamak what he has done to make girls love him. He had better teach the secret to Ramin and his brothers as well. Siamak answered seriously that it wasn't the right time for that sort of thing.

Ramin trusted Siamak when he sent him to Afsaneh's place, even though he still wasn't clear about his own feelings toward Afsaneh. Sometimes she seemed like simply a friend, other times something more. In the middle of the night he would wake with a strong desire to see Afsaneh. He never asked himself if he loved her, never uttered the word love. But to be with Afsaneh was like a sweet dream and at the same time a dream he was ashamed of. Perhaps because Siamak said it wasn't a time for romance. After he married Negar, Ramin believed he had to free himself from that shame. During these few days camping he had discussed this feeling with Afsaneh. She laughed, saying, "I wish the feelings of shame people have were more like yours, flavoured with love."

One early summer day in 1981 the Mojahedin rebelled and openly declared themselves against the Islamic Republic. A real war was declared. The government began widespread persecution, imprisonment and execution of political activists; both the Mojahedin and leftists. After this crucial day Ramin didn't dare to think about his feelings for Afsaneh. Perhaps the difference in their points of view created a barrier, made it too difficult to judge his own feelings. Perhaps the barrier was his faith in Siamak and in what his father had planted in him, since childhood. Add to that, Afsaneh's denial of what he and Siamak believed. Ramin knew Afsaneh's character, but he couldn't make other people understand her. On the two hikes when Afsaneh accompanied his group, her modesty, her helping hand, her kind personality were seen and acknowledged. Siamak couldn't accept her as a member of his group, and Afsaneh didn't show any willingness to join it. It was Ramin who insisted Afsaneh join, Ramin who encouraged her to accept their ideology. He talked about it to Siamak, and he believed it was worth working on her longer. Siamak viewed her as member of a class which had stood against the working class, generation after generation. He believed she carried the legacy of a decayed tradition, which had to be thrown away. She must change her ideology and her point of view. He advised Ramin that, because he couldn't be sure a basic change had occurred in her thoughts and ideas, he shouldn't trust her. Ramin should consider her an enemy.

The dispute between Ramin and Afsaneh was different. Ramin tried to explain his own ideas in grandiloquent language. He showed her quotes from famous philosophers and political leaders to impress her. Afsaneh disarmed Ramin with short answers that were mostly ironic, then changed the subject. Their discussion would heat up, and they would talk for hours. Then Ramin would give up, unable to withstand Afsaneh's challenges. Whatever she said, seemed reasonable. Ramin couldn't disagree when Afsaneh used examples from real life and the people around them. Ramin asked her, "Where did you learn so much?"

"From novels and from life," she answered. "Novels are the source of my knowledge of life. I have never been fascinated by the theories and ideas of philosophers. I believe there are as many ideas as there are people, and that bewildered me." She continued, "For me, the characters in novels sometimes seem more real than actual people."

She talked about Anna Karenina, her courage, her solitude and her love. She talked about Mme. Bovary, captive in a traditional and joyless society. She talked about Oblomov whose laziness and pure heart weren't acknowledged by anybody. She talked about Raskolnikov and his tormented conscience. She talked about Mergan, and her simple strength as a country woman. She talked about dozens of people who existed in her mind and in books, as if they were real people.

Her ideas impressed Ramin and he repeated them to Siamak. Siamak said, "Yes, there are people like her who don't have to worry about their daily bread, don't have anything to do but read novels. The novels of Dostoyesky, Tolstoy and other bourgeois writers reflect her way of life. But real life, the life and torment of the working class, isn't written in any novels. Their ordeals aren't summarized in a romantic story, but in their caked hands, which Afsaneh hasn't noticed or touched." Siamak dismissed Afsaneh's ideas. Whenever Siamak talked about her, Ramin felt upset. But he still pressed Siamak to let her into the group.

The Afsaneh he knew was different from the picture Siamak painted of her. Ramin knew Afsaneh came from a wealthy family, but being connected to a certain class wasn't important to her. Even though she was born into a rich family, she hadn't spent her life like a wealthy girl. Her childhood was like a short siesta which had become a vague memory. Then, with her grandmother she lived an ordinary life, a joyless life, until she was fifteen. Then she lived with Ozra. She told him that she had nearly finished high school before she went to a movie. She had no one to take her. In her last year of high school, she went to the cinema with her classmates. In France, she learned about serious films, then Majid Khan bought her a VCR and she was able to watch films she hadn't had a chance to see.

When Siamak knocked, Ramin was dressed to leave the house to meet Afsaneh. Ramin guessed something had happened between them. Siamak and Ramin went upstairs, and closed the door. Siamak blamed Afsaneh. He warned Ramin to end his relationship with Afsaneh, to be careful of her. Siamak argued late into the night that Ramin couldn't have a sincere relationship with a girl who lived differently and was a class enemy. Ramin couldn't understand why there was so much hate in Siamak's attitude toward Afsaneh. He didn't know if he was glad or angry that Afsaneh had sent Siamak away. He hadn't expected Afsaneh to be against Siamak. But he also hadn't expected Siamak to make a pass at her. For Ramin, Siamak was like a saint, free of sins. He wasn't supposed to lose control. Now Siamak was confessing that he had an instinctive attraction to Afsaneh and he had hugged her. Ramin felt strange pain and exultation, simultaneously. Siamak's anger at Afsaneh upset him. Siamak noticed and asked, "Why don't you say anything? Do you love her?"

The question Ramin had never asked himself. Something grabbed hold of his heart, warning him that this was serious, that he should ask himself.

Siamak stared at him.

"Do I love her? Of course I love her. She's my friend. I respect her, she's like..." He wanted to say, like a sister, he didn't.

"Are you in love with her?"

"In love?"

Ramin answered with hesitation, "I don't think so."

"Then leave her."

"Why?"

"I told you the reasons."

"It's not easy. She's a reliable friend. She understands me. I've learned a lot of things from her."

"Dangerous things."

"But I know another Afsaneh."

And without wanting to, just for Siamak's sake, Ramin said, "I even thought you might understand each other. Negar thought you might like each other."

"And you were worried."

"Why worried?"

"So you had that in mind when you sent me to her place?"

"Sending you to her place was Negar's idea. She thought you and Afsaneh..."

"So you set a trap for me."

"It wasn't a trap. Afsaneh isn't a bad person."

"She's a class enemy."

Ramin gave up. In these discussions, he was always the loser. Siamak, with his diatribes and theories, filled his head and silenced him. He preferred to be quiet when Siamak started discussing theories and political points of view. "If you considered her an enemy," Ramin said with unusual courage, "why were you attracted to her?"

"An instinctual attraction, an animal instinct," Siamak said, staring at Ramin's red face, "it wasn't my fault. She was there in a short sleeve dress, singing. She has a beautiful voice. The way she stood by the oven reminded me that she is a woman. In that moment, she was only a woman and I was a man. Two different sexes, with an instinctive attraction that was out of control. Male and female animals. Well, you see, it wasn't intentional. It seemed to me, she was tempting me. I was attracted to her and had to react. I wanted to tell her I had feelings like other people and could respond to her. I wanted her to know that my whole existence wasn't just theories and philosophy, as she believed, that I wasn't made of stone. I wanted to satisfy her desire."

At that moment Ramin was flooded with a jealousy and anger. He didn't know how to show this to Siamak. He only said, "And she sent you away."

"It's always the same, this is a natural reaction. The male sex is pulled to the female, but the female turns her back on him. As poets often say, a female protests and consents at the same time. It's the same in animals."

And Siamak talked again about class difference, about Afsaneh being dangerous, that Ramin better break off his relationship with her.

Siamak talked until late, stayed overnight. Every time Ramin remembered something he liked about Afsaneh, Siamak said something against her way of thinking and her ideas. Then Siamak talked about his problems. He was worried about Negar, who had become involved in politics very early. He said she wasn't ready for jail, hardship and torture. They must send her away from this dangerous situation. He proposed that Ramin leave Iran with Negar.

"You and Negar should leave Iran. Your safety is more at risk," Ramin said. Siamak answered harshly, "I have never thought of

leaving, and I never will. I'll stay until my last breath." He started
to talk politics again. He said that without responsibility, human
life has less value than the life of a worm. Human beings are born
to take responsibility. Great men always keep the flame of ideal-
ism burning and without them, human life would sink to the level
of animals.

Siamak's speech made Ramin feel estranged from Afsaneh.
His friendship, his special love for her paled, replaced by a feeling
of shame. He regretted sending Siamak to her place. That regret
intensified a few days later when Siamak was arrested in the street.
Ramin blamed Afsaneh for Siamak's arrest. He answered her telephone calls coldly.

On a brief visit, when Ramin went to Afsaneh's to pick up
Siamak's things, Afsaneh explained that she didn't blame Siamak.
She explained what had happened as Siamak had explained it. She
too believed it was an instinctive attraction. Ramin was sure she
was only saying that because of him, and because Siamak had been
arrested. She didn't want to cast blame on a hero, already considered a martyr by them all.

A few days later, in a restaurant on Darband Road, they talked
again of Siamak. Lost in regret over Siamak's arrest, Ramin blamed
her with veiled accusations: her short-sleeved dress, her singing,
those were the reasons Siamak grabbed her. Afsaneh was angry
with him, said he was thinking like the clergy, popular opinion had
affected him, he was saying that a woman should cover herself so
as not to provoke men. They finished the meal in bitter disagree-
ment.

Ramin never admitted to himself that he loved her. He didn't
recognize love. In the twentieth year of his life, he knew more
about politics than about feelings between a man and a woman.
Siamak had made a great impression on his life. It was Siamak who
taught Ramin Marxism and political philosophy. He had joined
Siamak's group, but wasn't yet active. Even though Siamak encouraged him to accept a specific assignment, Ramin didn't have

the nerve for it. He liked to contemplate something for a long time, deliberate on the different aspects of it. Whenever he was asked to do something, he asked himself: can I? He imagined the task would be too much and he wouldn't be able to handle it.

Ramin's father, Davood, a man of a soft temperament, discouraged him from action. In the last months before the revolution, people were enthusiastically attracted to demonstrations and slogans. Ramin, under Siamak's influence, became interested in politics. When Davood noticed his excitement, he spoke to him seriously. His father had been a leftist, a supporter of the Toodeh Party when he was young; he had spent a year in jail. When Ramin was younger, he had listened to his father and other party members trade memories of jail. Ramin's father and Siamak's father, Youness, had met in jail. Later, they became brothers-in-law and argued politics in front of their wives and children. The two men were alike in many ways. Unlike many old Toodeh members, who forgot about politics, went into business and exploited people just as the government did, both these men remained true to their ideas. And their only joy was to spend time together. In summer they would leave the city, read Persian classics like the *Shahnameh* and the poetry of *Hafiz,* drink wine and smoke. When they were almost drunk, they talked about their memories of jail.

Ramin had always known his father was opposed to the Shah's government. But his mother was a practical woman, indifferent to politics, poetry and literature. She was the elder of two sisters and married Ramin's father. She wasn't as pretty as her younger sister; she had married after Siamak's mother married. She treasured her family, devoting all her time to her husband and three sons. Her purity and sincerity had also left a mark on Ramin.

Unlike the old Toodeh, who were optimistic about the Shah's downfall and considered Khomeini's anti-American stand a big success, Davood was pessimistic. Defeat still disappointed him. Watching his former allies shed their principles to expropriate property alongside the Shah's regime taught him to distrust politics. He didn't agree with Youness about political theories. By the beginning of the Revolution the difference in the two men's ideas was clear. Davood sometimes refused to attend family gatherings, and criticized Siamak's extremism, saying it was necessary to stay out of fire or they, too, would get burned.

One day Davood sat Ramin down and spoke to him about politics and political games. He said politics had no place for humanitarian views or morality. "The end justifies the means," he explained, and that offered justification for the many political acts. People who wouldn't stop at killing their close friends, people prepared to lose their parents, their sisters, their brothers. Davood explained to Ramin that faith was the important thing in a fight. He asked Ramin, "How much faith do you have? What is your faith placed in? The world turns on force. Politics is a toy in the hands of powerful people. If you want to play the game, make certain you know what you're thinking and realize it's a game before it's too late. When you end up in the hands of the enemy, the enemy can manipulate you, make something of you so disgusting that you will disgust not only others but yourself as well. The most important thing is to be a human being. Be human first and foremost, regardless of your ideas and your way of thinking. As a human, you wouldn't be an executioner, you won't look at another man as nothing more than your enemy."

Ramin listened to him suspiciously and intensely. He repeated some of his father's comments to Siamak, who laughed and said, "Your father is getting old. The old are disappointed because they can't do anything. They become pessimistic."

But his father's talk gradually affected Ramin. He looked at his friends in the group. Most of them were extremists who boasted about themselves. He realized much of what his father said applied to them. But he was also influenced by Siamak and the current which carried them all. Ramin was part of the current, too. Davood's cautions moved him to greater respect and love for

Afsaneh. If the situation for political activists hadn't abruptly changed that summer, if Siamak hadn't been arrested, he might have had a chance at a closer relationship with Afsaneh. She might have met his parents and brothers. Davood's advice gradually weighed on him, and little by little Ramin lost his passion for political activities and became more cautious.

"Be careful my son. Choose your way with your eyes open. A big wave has arrived and everybody is in it. The wave is strong and pulls everyone with it. You have to keep your eyes and ears open. It's good to be part of a herd, to follow others along the same way, but if you are arrested, you won't have a herd or a shepherd. When you're arrested your friends may become your enemies. Experience has shown this can happen. I lived that. They look directly into your eyes as if they don't know you. Be careful my son, not to be one of them. Human beings are made of flesh and bones; under the skin lie nerves. You understand the function of nerves. You've studied biology. Push a needle under your nail and see how long you tolerate it. Your bones must be iron, your flesh leather and your heart a piece of brick. Or your faith so strong that it keeps you going. Otherwise it won't be easy. It won't be a joke. Open your eyes. Yes, a challenge is sweet, but it won't always bear a sweet fruit."

Davood's tone was bitter and cold, chilling Ramin to the core. His father didn't prohibit him from participating in politics, but Ramin lost his nerve and became cautious. It put a damper on the dreams Davood had planted in Ramin as a child. Ramin had wanted to be like his father, a man who cared nothing for worldly things, an idealist. It was suddenly confusing.

As Ramin got to know Afsaneh, he was amazed by how often and how deeply they shared sentiment. If half his existence was captive to Siamak and his ideas, the other half leaned naturally toward Afsaneh. Because he found Siamak so compelling and had relied on him so long, Ramin tied to convert Afsaneh to Siamak's ideas. But Afsaneh disappointed him. Her own logic was strong

and her refusal to accept ideologies she didn't believe in was stead-
fast. Ramin also noticed contradictions between the ideas and actions of political people. He remembered what his father had said,
but couldn't resist a movement that was spreading like wildfire.
Ramin admired Siamak, as a symbol of his beliefs. Finally he came
to the point where he accepted assignments when Siamak asked.
He did everything for Siamak. He didn't obey others whose actions belied their words. They called him a coward; this was a subject he felt ashamed to raise with Afsaneh. When Siamak was arrested, Ramin lost his delicate balance. His parents proposed he
marry Negar and leave the country. Later he told himself, "I just
wanted to flee. To escape that dangerous time."

In spite of childhood promises, as an adult Ramin recognized
the distance between Negar and himself. He sometimes told himself he should tell his parents he had decided not to marry Negar;
that he didn't want to don the robe they had made for him after
Negar's birth. But coming when it did, the proposal of marriage
to Negar calmed him. He would be free of the ever-increasing
pressure from Siamak's followers to take on dangerous assignments
and leadership roles. He could escape Afsaneh's friendship, which
now burdened him. She had exposed Siamak to arrest, but Ramin
remained eager to see her. The love and compassion in her eyes
captivated him, warmed him like a flame in a chilling time. But this
flame burned. He couldn't bring himself to dream of marrying
Afsaneh. "What would Siamak say?" Like a true charismatic leader,
Siamak cast a dominating shadow, a shadow both compelling and
tormenting. And Siamak had asked him to take care of Negar,
entrusted her to him.

A week after his marriage to Negar, Ramin went to see Afsaneh.
Afsaneh was surprised at the news, but he couldn't sense her true
feelings. These last few nights camping, Afsaneh had talked about
it. She said it seemed to her as if she had lost her dearest friend.
She wallowed in her pain and sorrow. That day, she had to stifle
her tears. Every time she went to the kitchen it was to hide her

tears. He had asked Afsaneh about life outside of the country and she encouraged them to go, saying for two young people like them, life wouldn't be hard.

"Why did you come back?" Negar asked her.

Afsaneh didn't answer clearly. She spoke to Ramin and ignored Negar. Later, Ramin wrote her a letter saying exile wasn't as she had described it. He regretted that he hadn't been able to find a friend like her and blamed himself for accusing her with regard to Siamak's behavior. He had written this letter two years they left. There were a few lines about Negar. Every day she became more charmed by the glitter of the new country. Working twenty-four hours a day, he still couldn't cover her expenses. Five pages of worries. Between the lines were hints about the hours he and Afsaneh spent together. He couldn't hide his regret about leaving, but there were no words of love. He wrote that she was the only true friend he had ever had.

Alone camping, Afsaneh explained, "When I got the letter I was in a bad situation. It was a few months after Firoozeh's suicide and I wished for someone to console me. I looked at the envelope. No return address."

"I didn't write my address, I don't know why. And then I didn't write again. To tell the truth, I didn't deserve you as a friend. I never did. You were two years older than me, two years that seemed like centuries to me. You were full of experience, as if you had lived forever. You had your own ideas about every aspect of life. I was a coward and a follower. I couldn't even be like Siamak, committed to politics. I was always on the sidelines and didn't have the guts to act. I was scared. Even now I'm scared. Since I left Iran, life has come crashing down on my head. Now I understand how carefree we were then. But this life is crushing."

Afsaneh put her hands around him and pressed his head to her chest. "No, my dear, you weren't a coward. You just feel guilty. Your choice wasn't your choice, others chose for you. You shouldn't have married so early. You and Negar are not made from the same cloth. Negar's parents used you as a shield for their daughter. They wanted to rescue her, but they left a heavy burden on your shoulders. You know that."

"I didn't then. I thought they were going to rescue me. They rescued me from jail and torture. I always put myself down. I wanted someone to count on me. I wanted Siamak to accept me."

"But you had an independent mind before marrying Negar. You used to say you didn't want to act without thinking and because of that you hesitated."

"Yes, I was afraid then, too. Fear stopped me. Marrying Negar and fleeing the country was a way of release. I accepted it, because I wanted be rid of my conscience which was tormenting me, and I wanted to be out of danger. But fleeing didn't change anything. Negar wasn't the one I needed. She's still the same spoiled girl. She thinks I have to look after her or she will break. I can't do it any more. It's beyond me. I'm not myself any more."

He walked along the dark road, lost in his thoughts. His past, his present, Afsaneh, Negar and Damon, were all ghosts in his mind. He stopped walking and asked himself, what am I going to do?

He turned abruptly, "I shouldn't leave her," he said aloud. "I left her once, and I paid for it. That's enough. I have to return."

"You think it was easy for me? You think I accepted your marriage and your departure easily? I had already decided to talk to you, but you were busy with Siamak. When he was arrested, you weren't yourself any more. I didn't dare speak to you. You didn't give me a chance, either. You avoided me, as if I had betrayed Siamak to the guards."

They were sitting on a bench close to the fire. Afsaneh put wood on the fire. The flames spread high, glimmering in the darkness.

"My love was like this fire, flaming and burning only in me, but it never went out. Perhaps Majid Khan was right, perhaps in our family love is a tragedy. I didn't believe him. I loved my father because he was in love with my mother. I respected him. Love isn't for everybody. All hearts don't deserve to be in love. I always waited for love, and then I met you, that day in the bookstore, do you remember? We went to a cafe, had ice-cream and then a pastry. How we talked! We quickly became friends, as if we knew each other from the past. It seemed I had found something very valuable. I didn't know it was love. I said to myself, I will never let him go. Sometimes I imagined you had the same feeling, too."

"I did, but I didn't want to accept it. Whenever I thought about you, someone in me said, do you love her? And I screamed at myself, no, I don't deserve her. She and I are from two different worlds."

"No we weren't. I didn't see any difference. I was you and you were me. But you didn't want to notice."

"The situation made me that way. If the times hadn't been like that, perhaps..."

"OK. That was the situation then. What about today?"

"The situation is the same. And there is the matter of responsibility."

I'm not just responsible for Negar and Damon, there's Afsaneh too. I shouldn't leave her alone. I'm afraid. Why didn't I insist more? Was I worried Negar would find out about my relationship with her? She'd find out, for sure. She might know by now. When she realizes that Afsaneh and I disappeared, she'll know. What's the matter with that? Let her know. I have to make my decision. I have to separate from her. Many couples separate. She might find a better man. She might be happy too.

It was a short meeting. Siamak had a few days of unshaven beard, a cap and sunglasses. Ramin hardly recognized him. He told Ramin hurriedly that all members of his group had been arrested. He was lucky he wasn't with them, or he would have been arrested too.

"Anyway it's not serious. I expected it. But I'm worried about Negar. She's too young to be involved in politics. I am making you responsible for her. She's a sensitive girl, modest and undemanding. Try to take her away, let her study. It was my fault. I didn't want her to be idle, to choose the wrong path for her life. I wanted her to learn about life. But well, you see, it's not possible. The situation changed. Now we have to get her out of danger."

One cold afternoon, Negar called him and told him Afsaneh had arrived from Montreal. When he arrived home, he didn't see in her much of the Afsaneh he knew in Iran. This Afsaneh was an exhausted, broken person. Negar guessed she had problems with her husband. That night she was quiet, amusing herself with Damon, sometimes wiping a tear from her eye. Late at night, when Negar and Damon were in bed, Afsaneh talked about her life. Ramin didn't understand clearly what her problem was with her husband. She talked about her futile expectation of pregnancy.

"He couldn't have a child or he didn't want to?"

"He couldn't."

"Might be an illness."

"No, he wasn't ill. He had himself sterilized."

"Sterilized? Why?"

"I couldn't understand very well. He told me he felt guilty. He considered himself a murderer."

"Why a murderer?"

She didn't say anything about Hanna that night, and the word 'murderer' stayed dimly in his mind. Over the following two years of Afsaneh's friendship with them, she didn't talk about Bahram, or her life in Iran. She said once, "My past is dead." She didn't let anyone else ask about her past, either. And if she hadn't spent these few days with him, Ramin would know nothing of Afsaneh's life without him. While camping, she pulled many curtains aside and let him see. She talked about her futile dream of having a baby, said Bahram knew and said nothing, just mislead her. She had loved a man whose hands were contaminated with the blood of an innocent girl. She talked about all this with tears in her eyes. Sometimes she couldn't even speak. She said her life after Ramin's departure had been hellish. Firoozeh and her painful suicide, Asad fighting Majid Khan, how it wasn't clear who Firoozeh's father was.

"You see, I hurt no less than you."

"But the point is I can't stay with you. Believe me. I'm not made for all this, I don't have the guts."

"Guts for what? Not to lie to yourself? To be yourself?"

"No, I'm not myself any more. I have to go back. I'm only myself in that house."

"You've let Negar take you by the reins and pull you around whenever she likes. You know very well she'll crush you. How long do you think you can continue?"

"That is the question. I promised Siamak."

"But it doesn't mean you should suffer all your life, deny yourself a life."

"I won't have a life with you either. I'll never have peace."

"If you think so, then go."

He had left and now he was returning. He was worried he wouldn't find the way back to the camp. The night breeze rustled among the trees. The moon softened the darkness. Mosquitoes stung his neck, face, and hands. He scratched them involuntarily. He blamed himself, he blamed Afsaneh. Afsaneh had overwhelmed him. He was weighed down again.

"Then go. Do whatever you want. Don't worry about me."

He was coming back to take Afsaneh with him. I shouldn't have left her alone. I know she won't be afraid, but I shouldn't leave her there. I have to bring her back. She has to get on with her life, as I do. She has to understand. I've explained everything to her. Surely she understood. I wish Negar would understand, too.

It was a year since they had left Iran. They were still in Turkey and couldn't find a way to enter a European country or Canada. Ramin liked the idea of Canada, Negar still wasn't happy about leaving Iran. She was sullen most of the time, not eating meals, complaining.

"Why did we come here?"

"You know better than me. We had to."

"I was very young, I knew nothing."

"You wanted to marry me."

"But this life, this disgusting hotel, these people, these Iranians! I want to go back. I'll die here. I miss Maman and Baba. I want to see Siamak."

He had hidden Siamak's execution from her, suffered his death alone without talking about it to anyone, for fear the news would reach Negar.

"You should be strong. For Siamak's sake you should be strong. He wanted you to leave Iran, to live in peace and study."

"I can't. I'm not made for this kind of life."

"When we get to Canada, all these hardships will be over. I promise you."

"I'll be dead before we get to Canada."

They had spent more than eight hours at the immigration office. A long line before them; refugees from Iran, Afghanistan and Latin American countries. Negar had recently miscarried and couldn't walk quickly. Ramin also walked slowly. They were still at the end of the line. The immigration officer was a white man with very blue eyes, he stared at them, wanting to dig into their lives. He repeated his questions like a prosecutor, showing his suspicions and exhausting them. Ramin talked about what had happened to them, imagining he could convince the officer. But it was useless. Obviously the man was unaware of the line between truth and fiction.

Finally Ramin had to explain that Siamak had been executed. Negar, hearing the news for the first time, fainted. The officer decided Negar's fainting was faked and interrogated them more carefully, which took more time. Later on, Ramin heard that many people who didn't have political problems, invented lies which seemed more truthful than what he said. These people easily crossed the refugee claimant bridge to enter Canada. His truth paled in comparison to their lies. He explained this to Afsaneh with a bitter smile.

The officer gave them the address of a hostel where they could spend a few days while finding a permanent place to live. It was February. The city had been invaded by a terrible snowstorm. The taxi drove along highway 401, heading east. Ramin was surprised to see the highway full of vehicles late at night in a storm.

The taxi driver let them off at the hostel. Ramin looked at the taxi's meter and, changing it to his currency, was astounded. For a long time he and Negar imagined the driver had cheated them.

It was two in the morning. A young woman with dishevelled hair, awakened from sleep, received them. When she said they didn't have any room, Ramin, who barely understood what she was saying, translated for Negar. Negar started to cry. The woman said they could spend the night sharing a room with a young couple and their baby. They accepted, and the woman led them to the room. A black man opened the door.

Negar was shocked and didn't want to go in. They spent the night in the office. Negar cried quietly and asked Ramin about Siamak's death. To calm Negar, Ramin said he had lied at the immigration office. All that night Negar didn't sleep, and didn't let him sleep either.

"Come on, have this coffee and cookie. If you don't eat, you'll get sick."

"What happened to them then? Didn't you call them?"

"You saw that I called. They didn't answer."

"You might have called a wrong number."

In the afternoon a teenage boy answered the phone and said his father was coming home late and his mother would be back at six o'clock.

"What are we going to do now?"

"We have to wait here, until they come. We don't have any place to go."

Negar cried again. The hostel employee looked at her and said something neither of them understood. Ramin insisted on going for a walk outside which looked beautiful in the winter sunshine — snow on the sidewalk, the tree trunks and the bare tree branches. Maria, the hostel employee, noticed them leaving the building, made them understand that they should have warm clothes like a scarf and hat. She warned them about the cold weather. Ramin and Negar didn't take her seriously. As they walked into the street, a freezing wind slapped their faces, attacking them like a savage animal. The street was still piled with last night's snow. A narrow path, the sidewalk for pedestrians, was covered with ice. They walked about twenty steps. Negar turned back. The cold penetrated them to the core. Maria gave them a meaningful smile and again said something else Ramin didn't understand. She made them understand that the clothes they had on weren't warm enough for the winter cold in Canada. She opened a closet with coats hanging in it. She talked to them with her hands indicating they could have a warm coat if they liked. Ramin chose an old suede coat with a lambskin lining. Negar looked at it with disgust and wouldn't let Ramin touch it.

"They just left us their old clothes," said Negar.

She held Ramin's hand and led him away from the closet.

Later on, she became a customer at second hand dress shops. Ramin protested — so many dresses — but she didn't listen.

Three hours later, Mr. Engineer Farhoodi arrived, saying his son had paged him with news of their arrival. Negar's father had given them Farhoodi's address before they left Iran. From Turkey, Ramin had written him a letter asking about life in Canada. Farhoodi answered his letter with two long pages about his year of experiences living in Canada and signed it, Mehdi. He encouraged them to look for a smuggler to get them to Canada as soon as possible.

At first glance Ramin didn't recognize him. This Mr. Farhoodi wasn't the same Mr. Farhoodi he knew in Iran. His hair hadn't been cut for almost six months. It was like a black mop mixed with gray on top of his head. He still had his fat moustache, but longer and bigger. He had on a heavy gray coat, a shirt open at the collar and a colourful sweater. His jeans were old and faded. He spoke and laughed loudly, as he had in Iran.

He laughed at the astonished faces of Ramin and Negar saying, "What is it? Don't you know me? It's me, Mehdi."

Mehdi looked strange to them. Nothing at all was left of Mr. Engineer Farhoodi in Mehdi, except he was still loud and cheerful.

"Mr. Engineer..." Ramin began.

Mehdi laughed loudly, saying, "Don't call me Mr. Engineer. Here everybody is called by his or her first name, even the prime minister."

Mehdi helped them put their luggage in the taxi then sat behind the steering wheel. Ramin and Negar hadn't imagined Mehdi as a taxi driver. Ramin slipped into the front seat and forgot he was sitting in a taxi.

They left a highway full of vehicles for a wide, long street with houses and high buildings on both sides. The city seemed to plunge into a dead silence. There was snow on the ground and on roofs. Mehdi talked all the way, educating them with his knowledge of the city and life in Canada. But it was as if the words were said in a vacuum; they didn't reach Ramin. He gazed out of the taxi at the houses, shops, and the few people in their heavy coats, becoming fewer as Mehdi drove on. Mehdi looked back at Negar, in the back seat. She wore a light leather coat, bought in Turkey.

"This is Canada. It's not bad, is it?" Followed by one of his loud laughs.

"What's wrong? You look upset."

Negar became herself again. Ramin turned and looked at her. "Are you cold?"

"She's cold, for sure, with that summer dress," Mehdi said. "This is Canada, land of polar bears." He looked at Ramin. "You know what Canadians are proud of?" Without waiting for an answer, he said, "The cold." Laughing loudly again. "If you live here for a while, you'll see these people always talk about the weather; whether it is hot, or cold, chilly or nice, wonderful or terrible. As if they don't have any worries except the weather." He looked over his shoulder at Negar. "And they really don't. You'll see."

Ramin stopped walking. He didn't know how far the park would be. Night had descended completely. The trees on both sides of the road were like black ghosts in the moonlight. He paused for while and looked back. The noise of the main highway was a buzzing that reached him from far away. He was lost and abandoned. It crossed his mind to go back to the main highway and return home. Afsaneh left his thoughts; Negar replaced her.

"Why are you crying? What have I done? I don't know where to go. We have to wait for Mehdi to come home."

Negar said nothing. She cried, she didn't eat, she complained about how much she missed Iran. She lay down on a sofa, hid her face in her hands, upset with him.

Mahboobeh, Mehdi's wife, showered them with advice from the moment of their arrival. The first few days, because of learning about Siamak's death, they looked after Negar. But that news, like much painful news from far away, soon lost its importance. Mahboobeh tested their patience. Negar made fun of Mahboobeh when she wasn't there.

"Is this the Canada you brought me to? You brought me here, to this cold country?"

The second week, they got their welfare allowance and Negar spent half of it buying warm dresses and a coat.

"You said that you know how to speak English, well then, look for an apartment for us."

"Well, I could. In Turkey I spoke English. Here, their accent is different. I can't understand them."

When they talked about finding a place, Mehdi commiserated, "I know it's hard for you. It was the same for us too. We stayed for two months with Saeedeh and Majid. Majid was a general manger in Iran, Saeedeh a chemistry teacher. Now Majid is my colleague, driving his own taxi which he calls Rakhsh, giving rides to people in this country. Saeedeh is lucky, she has a job in a bank. She's proud of her job."

"She has a right to be," Mahboobeh said, "she's not forced to stand on her feet the whole day."

"Oh yes, she has to," Mehdi said, "haven't you seen bank tellers? All of them are on their feet. It's not serious. One gets used to things. We were two months in their place. There were nine of us living in that tiny apartment you saw the other night. Don't be in hurry. It's hard to find a place in winter. When the weather gets better, you can buy most of your furniture at garage sales."

Then Mahboobeh gave a long speech about garage sales.

"Second hand furniture?" Negar asked.

"Perhaps older than second hand," Mehdi said.

Mahboobeh turned off the TV. Its noise had filled the living room. Sassan lay on the sofa eating chips. "That's enough," Mahboobeh ordered, "go to your room and go to sleep."

Sassan raised his voice saying, "Maman!"

"Don't you have any homework, child?" Mehdi asked.

Sassan had the bag of chips on his belly and was chewing it noisily, "No."

Mahboobeh said, "Go and get your homework. I want to see it."

"I don't have homework."

"Then go to sleep," Mehdi said.

Mahboobeh grabbed Sassan's arm and dragged him to his bedroom.

"You see, these children..." Mehdi said, laughing and didn't continue.

"What grade is he in?" Ramin asked.

"Grade five," Mehdi said, "but he never has homework. We can't force him to do anything. Here, it's different, there's no beating. If you punish a child they take the child away from you and give it to another family. But we're happy for Sohrab. He has found his way. He's studying computer engineering. I wish he would had stayed in this city, be a role model for this one. But he moved to Vancouver. He couldn't stand the cold weather. He got a scholarship and left."

A car was approaching from far away, its headlights glaring in his eyes. Ramin lifted his hand. The car slowed down, stopped beside him. He wanted to ask the way to the park, but he was tongue-tied. Words vanished and he couldn't form a sentence. The driver stared at him. A middle-aged woman was sitting beside him, wearing Hindu attire.

"Are you lost?"

Ramin gained control of himself and asked directions back to the park. The man put his hand out the window and pointed, saying something Ramin didn't understand. He could hear noises of tires on the road for a while, then they faded away.

Mehdi was happy and showed his joy with loud laughter and quick sentences. He had cut his hair and was wearing a red sweater.

Sometimes he gently slapped Sassan's or Mahboobeh's back. Negar had come back from the hospital and had three-day-old Damon in her arms, waiting for Ramin to bring the baby formula. Mahboobeh put a gift-wrapped parcel on the bed. She took Damon from Negar. Mehdi took a quick look at the baby and said, "You've finally made trouble for yourself. How often did I advise you not to do that?"

Ramin was torn between serving the guests and looking after Damon, curling in Mahboobeh's arms. Mahboobeh took the bottle of milk and put it in Damon's mouth.

"Guess what happened?" Mehdi said.

Joy was clear on his face and transmitted itself to Ramin. Ramin thought he might have won the lottory, a dream of his since he arrived in Canada, a dream which deceived many.

"Guess what?"

Mahboobeh, giving the baby a bottle, said, "He's a winner."

Mehdi's loud laughter convinced Ramin he had won. He wanted to embrace him but Mehdi said, "Much better than that. That's nothing."

Sassan was still standing in a corner of the room, with no place to sit. He said, "He's been accepted to college."

"College?" Ramin asked. And left the room. When he came back, he had two chairs in his hands and put them by Negar's bed. Sassan and Mehdi sat down.

"Yes, my boy," said Mehdi, "at last I can take a computer training course at government expense; a computer and drafting certificate. They say there is plenty of demand for those sorts of jobs." And again he slapped Sassan's back, who jumped up protesting. "From now on your father will be a student like you. Each morning you and I will go to school."

Ramin walked and forgot where he was going. A breeze touched his skin and dried his sweat. Afsaneh faded from his thoughts.

Negar and Damon were sleeping. Mahboobeh too. The campfire was burning.

"All other people get a job and celebrate," Mehdi said, "we lose our jobs and go camping to celebrate." He emptied a can of beer into a green mug, saying, "Drink it, drink to this world and this life, this system. They wouldn't even let me have a taste of office work. When I started to work, the recession began. We suffered from the recession not them. Last hired, first fired. And we're always at the end of the line."

"You see Ramin, it's like this. Someone wants to learn the customs of a new country and before they do, his or her life is over. You see how the years pass quickly, they fly past. I've been here six years and I'm still at the beginning. I can't believe it. I hope my children have a future. Sohrab has found the right way. This year he will get his Master's. I thought he might help us, but he's going to marry. It seems she is pregnant. I wish them happiness; we won't ask for anything. I'm worried for Sassan. He doesn't care about school. I don't know what to do with him. He doesn't listen to me or his mother. He refused to come camping. He might be right. Our world is different than theirs. But I'm afraid he'll take a wrong turn. Think about it. We uprooted ourselves for our children and things aren't turning out for them as we expected. You're lucky; you're young. Try to continue your education. Set aside poetry and literature, there's no future in them. Stick to the dollar. As for me, I have to think about something else. They didn't even let me get a taste of an office job. After barely a year, they laid me off."

The fire was licking the darkness. The forest sank into the night's silence.

"Yes, try to finish your education. Set literature aside. Choose a field that has money in it."

"It's not possible. You see, with this child...and Negar too, she is always sick."

"It has nothing to do with Negar. You just spoil her."

Ramin abruptly came back to himself. He was heading through the darkness, wondering if he had missed the park gate. A car came from behind; he lifted his hand. The car stopped, he saw a man and woman with a child in the back. He asked for directions to the park. The man said something to the woman which Ramin didn't understand. The car drove on. A bit further on he saw a lit-up area behind a bunch of trees at the park entrance.

The square was lit by high lamposts with bright white bulbs. The tall trees made a dark wall in the night silence and darkness flooded the rest of the camp area. The park employee, a young man with wavy blond hair, was in the office, sitting behind a desk by the window. Three dirt roads curved sharply into the trees. Ramin didn't remember which way they had gone in, or which way he had come out that afternoon. He stood for a while, trying to guess, and then chose the road to the right, walking into darkness. After about twenty steps, the path had a sharp curve, and darkness blocked his way. He heard a rustle among the leaves, warning him not to step further. He walked quickly back to the lit area. A park employee stood by the entrance door, talking to a driver of a white car with a canoe on the roof. Ramin stopped until the car passed, walked up to the young man, trying to remember the location of Afsaneh's tent. He asked for park directions. The employee found the place on a map on the wall and lent him a flashlight with a promise to bring it back in the morning. He said their tent wasn't very far.

Flashlight in hand, Ramin thanked the young man and chose the path to the right, heading through the darkness with a flickering light. The path broke in two suddenly and he chose the right one again instinctively, continuing to walk. A middle-aged couple were sitting on the bench in front of a fire playing cards. They stopped playing and said hello to him. He answered their greeting absent-mindedly, quickening his step as if they might stop him. Further ahead, the campsites were empty. Two nights before, on

the weekend, most of the campsites had been full. The smell of
wood fires and barbecues had filled the area. He looked for a tent
the colour of brick.

Afsaneh recited some of Shamlu's "Fairies" by heart, and he
recited too:
"Fire, Fire,
How fine it is
The time of sunset approaches
Night is not far away
Nor the feverish glow." Afsaneh learned her head on his shoulders.
"I wish I could stop time."
He didn't answer. He was thinking of Negar. Negar wouldn't
leave him alone for a second. The longer he spent with Afsaneh,
the more Negar imposed herself in his thoughts. He pressed
Afsaneh to his chest, as if he wanted to consume her like an in-
toxicating wine, but his thoughts were occupied by Negar.

"Why? We were supposed to wait a few more years. We were
supposed to finish school and then have children? Didn't you promise? Why didn't you say anything?"
"I knew you wouldn't agree. I'm twenty-two. When should I
have a baby? At fifty? My education may not be finished until fifty.
How many years has Mahboobeh been studying? In the beginning she used to tell us she would finish in two or three years. Why
didn't she? What about Mehdi? Why didn't he finish either? After
almost six years, Mehdi still drives a taxi. Mahboobeh is a cleaner
in a donut shop. Do you think studying is easy? I can't do it. You
saw how I became depressed. You heard what the doctor said, I
shouldn't do anything strenuous. Well what should I do then? The
doctor said I should have a baby. A doctor doesn't talk for the sake
of talking. You saw I was getting depressed."
"I won't take responsibility."

"As you like. You never take any responsibility. You brought me here with so many promises. Far from Maman and Baba, far from my family, to this cold country, to this exile, and now you don't want to take any responsibility. I'll raise the baby myself. To tell you the truth, I got pregnant on purpose. If you leave me, what can I do? Well the child is insurance for me. The government will help me, they won't force me to work."

A raccoon appeared in the darkness, looking at him surprised, then disappeared among the trees. He searched both sides of the road for Afsaneh's tent in the flickering light of the flashlight. He couldn't find it. Ramin could smell the lake breezes.

"I think I'm getting close," he thought. He walked faster, toward a sharp curve. Afsaneh's tent was at the turn in the road, he ran over to it, calling her. No answer. The zipper was open. He shone the flashlight. Afsaneh's purse and a few pieces of clothing were on the sleeping bag, still spread on the floor of tent. He called Afsaneh again, his voice echoing in the silence. A rustle among the leaves startled him. The moon was high. He walked through trees, climbed a small hill. The lake stretched out in the moonlight. Standing on top of a big rock he called Afsaneh. His voice echoed over the lake without an answer.

"She might have left." He returned to the tent area and this time noticed Afsaneh's car parked under a large tree, as it was last night and this afternoon when he left. He hurried to it, hoping Afsaneh was in it. He shone the flashlight on it, calling Afsaneh again but this time quietly, sure she was there. She wasn't.

She must be around, he thought, she might have gone to the washroom.

Ramin ran to the washroom. Stood by the women's washroom for five, ten minutes. A tall, white woman went in and came out. His certainty that Afsaneh must be there was gone. Still, he stayed there longer. Afsaneh could be anywhere. A medium-height woman in a pink sport dress came out of the washroom, holding a young girl's hand. Both of them had covered their heads with towels and had red shiny faces. The woman looked at him and asked, "Are you waiting for someone?"

"I'm waiting for my friend."

"But no one is in the washroom. What's her name?"

"Afsaneh."

The woman and daughter went into the washroom and called Afsaneh, pronouncing her name strangely. Silence. She called her again. Ramin waited. The woman's eyes were full of questions.

He went back. His hopes faded as he walked slowly, but he didn't want to give up hope. Maybe she had gone swimming.

"It's not frightening. The lake is the same day or night. At night it is even more beautiful. At night everything is quiet, rocks and water…"

"Tides occur at night."

"In oceans. Not in this small lake."

She threw herself into the water and began swimming. She stopped when the water reached her neck.

"Don't be afraid, come on, the genies have gone to a feast."

She laughed loudly, kissing him, and wrapped him in her arms.

Ramin turned back to the tent area.

"I shouldn't have left her. If I find her, I will never leave her. I don't care what Negar will say. I shouldn't leave Afsaneh." And Afsaneh was like a sigh leaving his chest and disappearing. Lost, gone, where, he didn't know. Afsaneh was a story now, like the meaning of her name: story.

"So, all the time you did this kind of work. Why didn't you study?"

"It wasn't possible. It wasn't easy."

"Did you try university?"

"I did. I passed the English exam, and took a few courses. But it didn't work. Too expensive to continue."

"Many people work and study."

"They do, but I couldn't."

The fire was burning. Afsaneh put pieces of wood on the fire. Both of them sat beside it on a bench. In the evening, there was a brief rain. The weather was cool. Wind rustled the leaves. They had on warm clothing and the fire warmed their knees. Afsaneh leaned on Ramin's shoulder. Ramin touched Afsaneh's hot knees.

"Negar didn't get along with me. She promised not to get pregnant until we finished school. But she didn't even finish high school. She didn't want to study. Well, it was hard for her. She isn't cut out for difficulty. Then she got pregnant, without letting me know. Like this second time. Well, with the baby, our problems multiplied to thousands. Expenses were endless. This society is like a sponge. Whatever you earn, it isn't enough. A person like Negar is never pleased with what she has. How could I study? I have to work sixteen, seventeen hours a day. It wasn't a joke. Sometimes I think of all the people I knew who accomplished something. For example, Mehdi and Mahboobeh. When we arrived, we went to their place. We stayed three weeks with them. This Mehdi, believe me, he didn't have a lot of self-esteem. He said he was afraid to go to school. He was afraid he wasn't capable, he would be ashamed in front of his wife and children. But he did it. His wife gave him confidence. Mahboobeh too, it took time, a few years longer than they imagined, but they did it. Now both of them have good jobs. At least their work doesn't embarrass them. Others too, they manage, they buy a house or have a business, get a degree or achieve something. It's only us who are still in the same place where we started. I don't even have time to read a book, I, who couldn't live without books. Who had such dreams.

Mountains in my hands
seas in my heart

sun, the light of my way
I think as high as the galaxies.

"You see it wasn't my fault. I couldn't bear it any more."

"You endured a lot. But it's over now. From now on, it will be just you and me. We will live as we like."

"Is it possible?"

"Why not? It depends on you. It depends on whether you want to or not."

"What about the children? Negar?"

"Your children are mine too. Don't think about Negar so much. She's an adult."

"But she needs my help. She can't handle life by herself."

"We'll help her as much as we can."

Ramin submitted to Afsaneh's kisses. Dreaming Afsaneh's dreams, he imagined himself alone with her. He wished he could live her dream, go far away, anywhere, not think about Negar, Damon. Cut off the last ten years of his life and connect it to that spring, the day he met Afsaneh in that bookstore. Meeting her, talking about their common desires. Tell her: "From the first moment I met you, something bloomed in me. I witnessed a renewal in myself. A rebirth. Yes, it was a rebirth." The words were in him but he couldn't speak them. What he voiced were his worries, his agonies. He was helpless to speak his inner thoughts. The first night and day, he was perplexed, confused and disturbed. He yielded to Afsaneh, listening to her talk. Sometimes he didn't hear her, didn't listen, but her voice was like music, like a breeze caressing him. Exhausted from making love with Afsaneh, he fell asleep. When he woke, Afsaneh was sleeping. He asked himself, "Am I dreaming?"

He had consigned Negar, Damon and Toronto to the past and wanted to forget them. They were like false memories he didn't want to think about. Something in him partially blocked thinking about yesterday or last month.

The fourth night, he revealed his heart to Afsaneh. He spoke about the hidden parts of his life, his suffering. He cried in Afsaneh's arms and fell asleep at dawn. He dreamed about Siamak. They were to meet on the street. He arrived before Siamak and waited for him for hours. Siamak didn't show up. Disappointed, he was returning home, then he saw Siamak at a curve in an alley a little farther ahead, talking to Afsaneh. He ran to them, joyfully, but they ignored him. He was hurt, a lump in his throat and tears in his eyes. He woke up and felt tears on his pillow. He opened his eyes and saw Afsaneh smiling at him. "Were you dreaming?" she asked.

"How did you know?"

"From your trembling face. It seemed you had a sad dream, you were crying."

It was morning. The birds were singing a triumphant symphony, filling the area.

"Do you hear it?" Afsaneh said.

"What?"

"The birds. As if they are doing their morning prayers. Morning prayer might be an imitation of birds singing."

He listened. But he hardly heard the birds' song. He listened to the dispute in himself. "I have to go back," he told himself. "No one will forgive me for what I've done. Not Negar's parents or mine."

"Why don't you say something? Did you have a bad dream?"

"Yes, I did."

"What was it? Tell it to me."

"I can't."

"Why?"

"I don't know. It was a bad dream. I saw Siamak in my dream."

He didn't want to say: you were with him too. Afsaneh sighed and said nothing. Whenever he talked about Siamak, she became quiet.

"Well, what happened?"

Ramin sat upright. Afsaneh lay down on her back.

"You don't want to tell me your dream?"

He looked at her. He didn't see Afsaneh, he saw Siamak, ignoring him, moving far away from him, with Afsaneh.

"If you were in Negar's place, how would you judge me?" he asked.

Afsaneh was quiet, still lying down looking at nowhere.

"Well? Tell me, how would you judge me?"

"Why do you think about her so much?"

"You're right. For a long time I've known that for her I'm nothing but a breadwinner. Sometimes I think she's miserable, too, clinging to me, living with me without love. I wish I could avoid thinking about her."

"You can, if you want to. Look at yourself, as Forough says, Behold. You never went on. You were drowned down."

"Do you think I can?"

"If you want to, why not?"

He eyed Afsaneh. Her words flowed like a cascade. She lay on her back, her hand under her head. Her big black eyes were shining in the pale pink light of the brick-coloured tent. Her face was smooth and gleaming. He had never seen her so beautiful. He held her in his arms, put his head on her chest, saying, "Oh Afsaneh, tell me what to do. What to do with this guilty feeling."

She lifted her head and looked at him; there were tears in his eyes.

"I dreamed about Siamak this morning. We had an appointment. I waited for him a few hours. When I was going to leave the place, I saw him standing with you talking. Both of you ignored me, your backs to me, and went away."

Afsaneh kissed his face. She took his head in her hands and wiped away the tears with her fingers. He pulled himself away from Afsaneh.

"I have to go back," he said.

Afsaneh sat up too.

In these few days, they hadn't mentioned the future. The future was the minutes and hours that were passing. There was no future. Time ended in those minutes, as if the world had reached its end, and beyond these days and moments there was nothing. Whenever they woke up, they drowned once again in each other's soul and body. They didn't want to speak about the days which would fill the next week or next month. On the fifth day at the campsite, it seemed as if they had lived a long time side by side. Hundreds of memories took root in their hearts. Sometimes it seemed they'd been together since they were born. They knew each other's secrets and became one in their knowledge of each other.

Ramin looked at her. "Why don't you say anything?"

"What can I say?"

"Talk to me, Afsaneh. Don't condemn me. I'm not evil."

"Please don't talk about leaving me. Don't say anything. Leave it for later on. Not now."

She kissed his whole body, made love to him. Whenever he opened his mouth to say something, she closed his mouth with long kisses. They fell asleep and when they woke, the sun slanted to the west, long shadows placed a cover of sadness over everything. Ramin opened his mouth to talk about leaving and Afsaneh listened in silence. She let him dress and prepare to leave. He was hungry, and took a piece of bread from the trunk of the car. Made a sandwich with bread and cheese. He gave half of it to Afsaneh. She took it and put it on the bench. He ate his bread and cheese, tried to talk to Afsaneh with logic instead of love. Afsaneh was quiet. She didn't argue or say anything. He imagined she had accepted his departure. And he left.

Ramin sat on the picnic bench and leaned on the table. The half-burnt logs, and the ashes spreading around were from last night's fire. The bread and cheese sandwich, the pot they boiled water in, to make tea, were on the bench. The moon lit the area.

The tent seemed darker, redder and lonely under the trees. Everything was part of Afsaneh. Afsaneh herself was like a sad tale, in his memory, like the years when they were separate, when he never believed he would see her again. Afsaneh was lost in this forest. Finding her again seemed like a miracle. He didn't expect any miracle. Afsaneh was just a story now.

The moon appeared among the trees, shining through the foliage. Each night, at this time, they had been in the lake, like two fish sinking into the water. Afsaneh moved her hands above the water, as if she was worshipping something. She was remembering Ozra. "Ozra always talked to me about genies. She said genies dance at night. If someone dances in darkness, she dances with genies."

They danced together.

"Where are they? No sign of genies. Why don't we see them? Maybe they are afraid of you."

"Of me? I'm half genie. Or whole. Yes, I am a genie. I wish I was. I wish we could become genies, you and me, and nobody could see us, living forever in this lake."

"What about winter? When this lake freezes?"

She laughed loudly.

"What's the difference? Genies don't feel cold or heat." She sank into the water, shouting, "Follow me."

Ramin got up, lighting his way through a narrow path among the trees to the lake. He stood by the lake. The moon shone in a vast sky. Small waves were shining in the moonlight. Nothing disturbed the silence and calm. He watched the surface of the lake. He hoped against hope that Afsaneh was somewhere in the lake, calling for him.

"Come on. Don't be afraid. The water is warm."

"Aren't you afraid to be left alone?"

"No, why should I be? I wasn't afraid last night or the night before. The lake is safer than the forest."

He couldn't take his eyes off the water. He stared in the distance. "She might have swum way out."

Far away, a light moved on the lake. When it came closer, he saw it was a canoe with a small engine. The light changed direction and went away. The engine noise disappeared into the lake silence. There was something on the water. Afsaneh, he thought, nobody except her would be in the lake at this time of night. Joy took him like a sudden storm. He threw himself into the water. He reached Afsaneh, out of breath, and realized he hadn't taken off his shoes. Afsaneh recognized him and laughed loudly, wrapped her hands around his neck, pulled him under the water. He swallowed a few gulps of water, and tried to pull Afsaneh out. He struggled to pry Afsaneh's hands from his neck. She was heavy on his shoulder. There was nothing under his feet. Fear of death and the heaviness of Afsaneh paralyzed his tongue, drained his strength. He spoke to her in his mind.

"Afsaneh, it's me. I've come to stay with you. Don't be foolish, Afsaneh. Help me swim. Afsaneh, I'm scared."

A small island, small as the backyard of a house; a rock with several trees was silhouetted in the moonlight close by. It seemed as if the island had risen up to give them refuge. Ramin pulled Afsaneh. The island was just a few meters away. The moon shone. The trees were still, motionless, like a painting with a cool sky in the background and the lake stretching around it. To the east, a faint light etched the horizon. But the sky remained black, with stars flickering happily. The incredible, terrible beauty shocked Ramin. He cried out, trying to bring Afsaneh back to herself.

"Afsaneh look, please, just look. How amazing it is! Look at the island. It's risen up from the water for you and me. A little island, a piece of soil, a rock, like a little house for you and me. Afsaneh, look, look at the moon, it's going to disappear. Look how big it is, how beautiful, how mysterious. Afsaneh, help me reach the island."

❧ FOUR ❧

༄ I happen to be tired of being a man. ༅
                              Pablo Neruda

BAHRAM SLIPS OUT OF HIS small tent. The sky is covered by gray clouds, the leaves a bright green. They remind him of Afsaneh, as if she was among the trees, watching him. The cabin sits silently and glumly surrounded by greenness. Silence dominates the area. He strolls to the cabin, opens the door; it's empty. Have they gone? Where? Why didn't I hear them, he wonders. Was that noise at dawn, them? I thought it was the neighbours waking early.

It's late morning; almost eleven. Bahram sits on a bench, wondering what to do. It's windy, the wind rustles among branches, threatening him. He remembers something Negar said about Afsaneh's wheat and lentils and how they were all rotten. Afsaneh had to throw them away, and predicted disaster. Negar mentioned it again last night and refused to go sailing with him. Is it possible? No, nothing happened to them. They've gone for a drive around the park or to the playground.

Bahram hears a car approaching. He listens. Is it Negar? The car drives away, a white car with a canoe on the roof.

"Where has she gone?" he mumbles. He's restless, he enters the cabin and looks around aimlessly. The beds are unmade. Children's clothes are strewn on the bed and the floor.

"They left in a hurry." He opens the fridge door. Fruit, and the meat for a barbecue are still there. A bottle of whiskey, half full. Tempted, he takes a big gulp. His throat and stomach burn. He's flushed with alcohol and anger.

"Stupid woman! Did I really want to drown her? Her and her

children? No. I wouldn't. But, I might have. Last night I was plan-
ning it. What kind of life is this? If she had gone sailing with me,
I'd have done it. Did she leave?"

Bahram can't believe Negar decided to leave on her own. "How
could she take Afi with her, my little Afsaneh?" He likes to take
the baby in his arms. She's the only one who calms him. Every
morning, he wakes up with the desire to hold her, and now...

Bahram can't calm down. The missing baby hurts. She is everywhere. He hears the sound of her laughter. Her pink dress is on
the bed. Negar has forgotten it, and the talking doll Afsaneh liked
so much. She laughed when it talked.

"Stupid woman! How dare she?" Those butterflies hanging
above her bed, how Afi enjoyed when they moved. She moved
her hands and legs, trying to reach them.

Bahram leaves the cabin. In the silent forest, he feels the absence of Negar and the children. Anger burns in him. He chose
to spend a week camping to relax, far from the tedium and futility
of life in the city, to reunite with Afsaneh at the lake, to be close to
her again. He rented a comfortable cabin for Negar and the children and a canoe with which to enjoy the lake. He didn't plan to
drown himself and them. No, not at all. Then, last night, the idea
crossed his mind.

"Was I crazy?" Perhaps. Negar had realized it. She wouldn't go
canoeing. He might not have done it. He wasn't sure he could do
it. But the idea persisted. He might not have had the nerve to do
it. He didn't know what he wanted to do. Negar said he was drunk.
He probably was. He didn't know.

Bahram imagines Afsaneh watching him. Hiding somewhere
among the trees. The leaves are rustling. Is it Afsaneh, or her ghost?
I know she's somewhere. Come out of the lake to watch me, watch
me with contempt. She knows how worthless I am. No, I'm not
worthless. Negar admires me, she counts on me. I only have to
touch her and she becomes a purring kitten.

He's still the tall, wealthy Bahram he used to be. He can be happy. He can take up his life again, start over again with Negar and the children. He has two children. "You see Afsaneh, how happy I am. Don't look down on me."

He's sitting on a bench, dizzy with alcohol and disturbing thoughts.

"They've gone. That incapable Negar found her own way and left me alone. Well, I did my best. Afsaneh, you witnessed what I put up with from her during the last year, but..."

The idea came to his mind, and the idea wouldn't leave him alone. He enjoyed thinking about it. He would do it. No, he shouldn't. I should drown myself. Everything is so ridiculous. Life itself is ridiculous. I wish I could end it."

Bahram didn't want Behnaz to drown. It was just that he hated her. His father used to say, "I wish Behnaz was a boy." Behnaz was supposed to have been his little brother. He had three sisters, older than himself. Three, who loved and obeyed him. Behnaz didn't love him. She should have been his brother. She was born with the hope that she would be a boy, but she was a girl, a sister. A sister who made fun of him, bullied him. And he didn't love her. He didn't want her to exist. But he didn't drown her. A wave took her away. He was close to the shore.

Did it make him happy? No, no, no, he cried. He screamed, and all night he had nightmares. For many years, whenever he remembered it. No, he didn't remember it. He tried not to re-member it. He was taken to a psychologist and the doctor made him believe it wasn't his fault. Afsaneh, too, said the same thing. He was just nine; Behnaz seven and a half.

"I have to finish it. I have to drown them with me. I shouldn't leave children behind. I don't have to love another man's chil-dren."

Negar realized and fled. He imagined Negar was stupid, but she wasn't. She realized he was crazy. Crazy? No, not quite. He can start again. There's always another chance. Start over. How old is he? Not forty yet. Why does he feel so old? How long is it since Afsaneh left him? Two years, three years. No, just a few hours. He went mad. Crazy about Afsaneh. Afsaneh made him crazy.

Bahram watches her. She has a loose, long, beige manteau, with big padded shoulders and a light brown scarf on her head. Part of her hair has fallen out of her scarf. How courageous she is! A few days ago, *Hezbollah* rushed into the streets and cut improperly veiled women with razors. Spat at them, took them away for strapping. She has a keen eye and stern features. She's talking with the general manager. Bahram can see her profile. The general manager introduces her to the employees. Bahram watches her from a distance. Nearing him, she looks directly into his eyes. His heart sinks. He remembers Hanna. For no reason, he remembers Hanna. He reddens and stutters. The general manager introduces him to her.

"Bahram Sedarati, educated in Canada."

She looks at him. A strange curiosity in her eyes makes him tremble. Her smile is generous.

"Canada?" she asks

He nods. She turns away. Her eyes dart everywhere. She walks on with the general manager. Her presence has left a mark on him. He's charmed.

"I know the genies. When I was a child, they were my playmates."

The following week she starts work in his office. He watches her whenever he can. Follows her with his eyes. They gaze at each other. She senses he's following her with his eyes.

The girl behind the counter watches him. Her big pupils are amazing. Her skin is the colour of burnt halvah, the sweets his mother made on the last Friday of every year and sent to the neighbours with Nanny Afagh. Nanny Afagh took him, and not Behnaz with her. Behnaz only accompanied them against Nanny Afagh's will. She'd make a face at him and followed them, crying.

He sips the last drop of his tea, still hungry. The girl says something he doesn't understand. She motions him to the counter.

"Are you a foreigner?"

"Yes."

"A Muslim?"

"Yes."

"An Arab?"

"Iranian."

She makes him understand that he can give her his teapot to fill again with hot water, without paying more money. He does it every night.

"If you wait a few minutes, my shift will be over."

He waits for her. He pretends to be reading. In Iran, he studied French for six years, but here, the accent is different. He can't speak fluently and has problems understanding.

It's October, the forecast is for snow. The coat he has brought from Iran is light. The cold makes him shiver.

"You should wear warmer clothes here."

She's sitting on the edge of the bed. Bahram is bewildered. He's sitting on the only chair in the room. Hanna is smiling.

"It must be hard for you here, far from your family. How long have you been here?"

"Five months."

"Do you have any sisters or brothers?"

"Three sisters, no brothers."

"So you are a beloved only son."

He nods. Hanna smiles. Her white teeth shine in her burnt brown complexion. A flame of desire flushes his face. Hanna moves closer to him, holds his face in her hands. His body is burning; his hands, like two limp branches, are on his knees. Hanna touches his lips with hers, and all her sweetness flows into his body.

When he regains himself, Hanna has left. In the light from the street, the room is like a cradle abandoned to eternity, transporting him to paradise. He feels weightless, pleasure flows through his veins. The nostalgia has left him, the cold doesn't sting, the lessons flow like water, he learns them easily. The streets, the buildings, the people are no longer foreign. In the evening, he flies to the donut shop, eats his soup and tea and is still hungry. Hanna gives him donuts or sandwiches when the shop owner isn't looking. He makes an appearance of studying until Hanna's shift is over. Hand in hand, they go to his place. Hanna's arms are full of kindness and warmth.

"Was it so easy? I can't believe it."

There is hate and disbelief in her eyes as she stares at him. Bahram wants to say, Afsaneh, don't judge me so quickly. I wasn't as guilty as you think. I was only twenty. I didn't know anything. Hanna shouldn't have been pregnant. My father forced me. But he's silent.

Afsaneh is quiet. He wants her to say something. He wants her to curse him, punish him, something no one has done. He's never talked to anybody about Hanna. He eliminated Hanna from his life, banished her from his thoughts. But Hanna stayed, somewhere in a corner of his mind. The day he met Afsaneh, Hanna revealed herself. Hanna made him blush. He should have known she wouldn't leave him.

There is disgust in Afsaneh's eyes. Afsaneh, don't judge me so harshly, he thinks. Have mercy on me. Don't curse me. Believe me, I didn't want it to happen like that. I liked Hanna. I wasn't in love with her, but I liked her. I treated her with respect. She had integrity. She was independent. She loved me like her own.

Afsaneh is still watching him. "Afsaneh, believe me..."

"What do you mean?" Afsaneh says, "you betrayed the poor girl with a baby in her belly."

I didn't, he wants to say. My father did.

His father is happy, and talkative. He leaves the gifts from Iran on the bed, looks around the room, sympathy on his face.

"We have to do something about your place. I'm going to buy an apartment for you. Do you have any idea about prices?"

Apartment prices? No, he hasn't thought about those kind of things. He spent his time studying hard, and passed the exams with good marks. Hanna helped him with the language. Hanna is a second year student, in sociology. She wants to be a social worker.

Father teases him, "Who's this lucky girl? When can I see her? You aren't supposed to commit yourself to a wife so quickly, to squeeze your hands and feet into a tiny walnut shell. But, well, a wife and children make a man responsible. Your mother was very happy, too. She wanted to come with me. I didn't bring her; the airplane tickets are expensive. She's happy you will bring her a blue-eyed grandchild. A blond daughter-in-law and a plump, blond grandchild."

His heart sinks. He hasn't explained to his father that Hanna isn't blond and blue-eyed, descended from generations of Europeans in Canada. He hasn't had the nerve to talk about it. Now he still can't. He looks at his father in silence. The gifts are on the bed. A gold embroidered vest for Hanna.

"Fereshteh sent it for your wife. This Baloochi dress is sent by Behjat. These earrings are from Nargess. Your mother sends this turquoise necklace."

Father shows him the gifts and Bahram wonders what to do with them. Reluctantly, he collects them and puts them in the closet. He thinks of Hanna. He wishes she wasn't that beautiful brown black. Wishes her skin could change colour overnight.

His father asks, "Why are you so quiet?" His father stares at him. He has realized something is wrong. "Is there something you're hiding from me?"

"I have to tell you something before you meet Hanna."

"What?"

"Hanna is an Arab."

"Arab? What do you mean?"

"Hanna is Black."

"Black? Like a piece of charcoal?"

"Not so dark, but..."

"But what?"

His father's growling. He still wants to see Hanna. He's angry and has lost his enthusiasm. When they meet in the restaurant, his father answers Hanna's greeting coldly. She takes her overcoat off. She has a red dress on, with an open collar. The red of her dress is perfect against her skin. His father is sullen. He looks at Hanna and Bahram with contempt. Bahram wants to say, Father, be polite, at least in Hanna's presence." But he doesn't.

Dinner finishes in a silent chill. Hanna barely touches her food. She can't swallow it. Sometimes she has tears in her eyes, but she tries not to release them. As she leaves the restaurant, there is a lump in her throat.

There's disapproval in Afsaneh's eyes; humiliation in his father's eyes; anger and disappointment in Hanna's.

"Was it so simple? You obeyed your father like a slave?"

He says nothing. Yes, he carried out his father's will.

"Let her go. Your mother asks for a blond daughter-in-law and a blue-eyed grandchild, and here you are with an Arab from Africa."

In the dim light of the street lamps, he can see only her white teeth. Hanna melts into darkness. Bahram fades into darkness as well. Her warmth flows in his veins. He opens his eyes and sees

Hanna staring at him. His arms are wrapped around her. Hanna's hands caress him, a breeze is blowing on him. He wants to be one with her. He presses her to him in silence. She accepts him. Her arms make the cold bearable. She slides quietly out of his arms. When she leaves, Bahram is sleeping. Hanna flees like a dream. He asks, "Why don't you stay?"

"My mother doesn't want me to," she answers.

She takes Bahram to her home. Her mother is tall and thin. She has bony cheeks and a skinny face. She reminds him of rural women back home. She has a colourful scarf on her head knotted at the back; her hair is covered by the scarf. In her face tiny wrinkles stretch over bone. She holds skinny, long fingers toward him. Her eyes talk more than her tongue. She wants to know everything about him. Hanna is three months pregnant. He doesn't know if she has talked about it to her mother or not.

He's worried. He didn't want Hanna to get pregnant, and doesn't have the courage to talk about it to Hanna. He's afraid Hanna will leave him. He doesn't dare encourage Hanna to have an abortion. Hanna is happy being pregnant. She introduces Bahram to her father. Her father has a tiny body, and unlike her mother, greets him coldly. He shakes hands formally. He's quiet during lunch, and looks at Bahram suspiciously. He asks about his family, and speaks French better than the mother. He asks about his religion. When Bahram says he's Shiite, he says nothing. He behaves coldly to Hanna, too. Bahram realizes the father doesn't like him or trust him. He counts the minutes, waiting to leave Hanna's house. The next time she invites him, he makes excuses and refuses to go. Hanna realizes he doesn't get along with her family. She's still full of love and desire. At night she stays late with him, and helps him with his courses.

"My belly is growing big, we have to do something."

He wants to ask, what? The question seems ridiculous to him.

"I talked about it to my mother. She says we should get married quickly; if father finds out about it..."

"Get married?"

He hasn't thought about marriage. He calls Iran. His mother answers the phone. She talks to him as if she is talking to a child. He tells his father he's going to marry. The loud laughter of his father bothers him.

"You? Marry? Your mouth still smells of mother's milk!"

"Father, you should..."

Father says, "Wait for me. I'll be there in a couple of weeks."

Afsaneh looks at him, her head above the water. Both of them are there: Ramin and Afsaneh. They are probably making fun of him. They laugh at his fear and weakness. "Coward! Coward!" But he acts in time. He's not a coward

"Why don't you want to get married at the city hall? We need only two witnesses. We have to marry because of my parents."

He wants to say, get rid of it. She reads his thoughts.

"It's late for an abortion. I don't want to have one anyway. I want to have my baby. Your baby, a handsome boy, like you."

"Like me?"

Mother takes him in her arms. Fleeing Behnaz, he's taken refuge in his mother's arms. Behnaz calls him, "Maman's boy". She destroys his toys.

"Have you hurt my pretty son again, you ugly Behnaz!"

Behnaz cries. Nanny Afagh picks her up and takes her away. Mother presses Bahram in her arms. The smell of his mother's bosom fills his nostrils. But Behnaz's voice stays with him.

"Coward! Coward!"

"Shouldn't your father be here too? Are you afraid to be alone with me? If..."

"If, what?"

What if father won't accept Hanna? Bahram is doubtful. He hasn't mentioned Hanna's background. That she isn't European. "Black? Arab?"

In his father's eyes, scorn.

Clouds cover the sky. Last night the weather was wonderful. Negar didn't want to go with him. What if she did, if the four of them had gone sailing?

Was it clear something might happen? Nothing would have happened. If he wants to, he can go and bring them back. Kiss her, buy her a piece of jewelry or a dress. She would come. Yes, he could probably go and bring her back. After him, who would take care of her and her children? His little Afsaneh.

No, he can't stand them any more. He can't stand anyone. He can't stand himself. Let her go and live as she likes. It's not the end of the world. There are millions like Negar on this earth. He's not responsible for them. But how can he abandon little Afsaneh? He witnessed her birth. He couldn't believe naïve, weak Negar could have such strength. It was like a miracle. That Hanna should have borne such a hardship, without a man beside her. A fatherless baby.

He took care of Negar. Stayed with her all through the delivery. The nurses assumed he was the baby's father. The real father.

"Come on, here is your pretty, healthy baby. She weighs seven pounds, eight ounces."

Negar is happy, her face covered with the sweat of exhaustion and pushing. Her eyes glittering. Afsaneh is born. From now on his life will be meaningful. There is a reason for living. He lifts her into his arms; she looks like a sparrow. He kisses her, and wants to cry. He remembers Hanna. He kisses Negar, too. She cries, too. Probably remembers Ramin.

Ramin? No, he doesn't think so. She's forgotten Ramin. She told everybody that Bahram is the real father of the baby. Well, he is. Isn't he?

"Pregnant? We just..."
She cries, "It's Ramin's."
"So you were pregnant? Why didn't you tell me earlier?"
"I felt shy."
"Shy? Why?"
"Well, I don't know."
He kisses her. He convinces himself the baby is his. He has been sterilized.

"I'm sterile."
"Sterile? How do you know that?"
"I know. I had it done."
Afsaneh's eyes widen with astonishment.
"Why?"
"It's a long story."
"How long? I'd like to know."
"If you promise not to leave me."
He drains the last drop of whiskey into his throat. Afsaneh doesn't believe him. She's heard Hanna's story from Sussan, Bahram's cousin. Sussan told her a Black girl was pregnant by Bahram. He wanted to marry the girl but his father made him change his mind. Afsaneh tells Bahram to see a specialist. He refuses, making excuses; he doesn't believe in them. She tells him she wants a baby so badly. He swallows another gulp of whiskey. He can't catch his breath and he coughs. He doesn't know how to begin. Hanna is with him day and night. Afsaneh and Hanna nag him to tell the truth.

Afsaneh screams at him, "Leave the crap aside. Tell me what you have done to yourself?"

He throws himself in Afsaneh's arms saying, "I can't. It's hard."

She separates from him. Looks at him coldly. "Tell me what happened? Otherwise I'll..."

He doesn't let her finish. Before he says anything he knows she'll leave him. He says, "I had to."

It's sunny now. The sky is clear and the clouds have drifted to a corner of the sky. The sky is a pure blue. "If Afsaneh were here. She is here. Afsaneh is among the trees, under the water, somewhere close to me. Afsaneh never left me. She's with me like an invisible genie."

He feels hungry, his stomach hurts.

There's ground beef in the fridge. If Negar and the children were there, he'd make a fire and hamburgers for them. He's not in the mood to make food for himself. He eats the plain bread and it tastes good. So, life goes on. In spite of everything, this bread tastes good. Death is far away. He chews the bread slowly.

He's coming home with Nanny Afagh. Nanny Afagh has two fresh, hot loaves of bread. She gives him a piece. The smell of fresh bread fills his nostrils.

"Why do you eat plain bread?"

"I like it. It reminds me of my childhood."

Hanna is sitting in front of him. She's made *gheimeh* sauce. But it has only a faint taste of a real *gheimeh*. The split peas are over-cooked, and mushy. It looks like a sauce without ingredients. Bahram laughs at her pronunciation of *gheimeh*. She eats her food with her mouth closed. He eats with gusto. Hunger makes his stomach ache. He swallows everything. Hanna gets up to clean the table. He pulls her to him, sliding under the blanket. Her body is as warm as the Caspian Sea on a summer day. He is drowned in her body's warmth. When he wakes up, Hanna has gone. She's washed the dishes, cleaned the table, and tidied the room. He sits by his desk and studies. He studies until late at night. He goes to bed at dawn. A sweet sleep flows through his veins, satiates him. He's alive and alert. The French language and his college courses aren't a problem. His marks are excellent.

He eats a package of pita bread and still feels hungry. He's empty inside. His heart is empty, his soul is empty. There's a big lump in his chest and throat, he breathes with difficulty. He's completely drained. A car sounds in the distance. It might be Negar. "If she comes back… no, she won't. She knew the plan I had. It was her fault. I'm glad she left."

He can go and bring her back. What if she goes to the police?

Bahram opens the door. Two policeman are there. One looks Iranian. A wheat-coloured complexion and tall. The other one is white, with a big body. He fills the doorway. He begins to speak, says Bahram's name. Bahram is surprised. What do they want with him? He thinks they have made a mistake. Bahram Sadarati?

He says, "That's me."

The police officer says, "Come with us."

Bahram wants to asks where, but he can't speak. He wants to ask, has he committed a crime, an offense? What? On the way the one who looks like an Iranian asks him, "Do you know Hanna Jamil?"

"Yes."

Through the streets of Montreal, he imagines everyone watching him. He stares ahead. There's contempt in the officers' eyes. What has he done? Who has complained about him? Is it Hanna? Where are they taking him? Jail?

The hospital room, with its white, cold walls. Its silence presses on his heart. Hanna is lying on a bed. Hanna? A policeman pulls the sheet aside. Yes, that's Hanna. Hanna is sleeping on the bed, calm, relaxed. Why on a hospital bed? He's standing back, doesn't have the courage to walk closer. He's a stranger to Hanna. It's almost six months since he heard from her. She doesn't work in the donut shop anymore.

"Do you know her?"

"Yes." He could have said no. Could have said, "No, I don't know her." And if he had said no, what would have happened? But he confirms he knows her. The policeman covers Hanna's face. Hanna is still sleeping quietly, sleeping forever. He's confused, he doesn't know where he is, where the hospital is. The policeman takes him back to his place, and tells him to come tomorrow morning to the police station, to decide about his daughter.

The policeman's tone seems sarcastic to Bahram. My daughter?

A Black? An Arab? How dare you bring her to Iran, to your family? "I don't want her."

"Are you sure?"

"Yes."

The policeman asks, "Are you her father?"

He wants to say, no, the baby isn't mine. But Hanna has left a letter, explaining everything. The letter is with the police.

The policeman says, "If you don't want the baby, there's a family who will adopt her. A family who were the mother's friends. They have promised to adopt her. They have a son and a daughter, and want the baby. The baby would have a respectable and reliable family."

He says, "Give it to them. I'm a student."

He signs the papers and leaves the station. The city seems strange. He has to get away. He sees Hanna's face everywhere. Behind every counter, looking at him with a cold smile.

"She killed herself with sleeping pills. No one is legally responsible for her death. Why didn't you marry her?"

The police officer's question.

"Why?"

Black? Arab? How do you dare bring her to Iran? Aren't you ashamed? What would your mother say? Your sisters? The relatives? Forget about her.

The police officer waiting for an answer. Bahram is confused.

"No one is responsible for her death."

A bird is singing beautifully. If Afsaneh was here, she'd probably read poetry. He's dizzy, just another gulp. He has made a promise to himself that he won't get drunk. He's not. How much then? The bottle was more than half full and now there's just one gulp left. The alcohol makes him bright, bright like the sun, like the morning, like the darkness. What? Darkness? He's like a mad man, spewing nonsense. Crazy? He's not crazy.

"Who goes sailing at night?" Negar says, "I'm afraid. I'm not coming. I won't let you take my children."

"What are you afraid of?"

She doesn't answer. Her eyes are full of fear. Idiot Negar realized the plan. He wants to take them on a long voyage. Damon is looking at him. He hates the boy. He looks like Negar. An intelligent and sensible child. He's spoiled. His father spoiled him for sure. The child understands that Bahram doesn't like him. Damon wants to do something so Bahram will love him. He wants Bahram to take him in his arms as he does Afi, but Bahram hates him. He hates everybody, he hates Afi too. No, he doesn't. He loves Afi. He witnessed her birth. He bore all the suffering with Negar, holding her hands in his, helping her deliver the baby. His dear Afi, his dear Afsaneh has been born. Afsaneh, oh, Afsaneh.

It's three months since Afsaneh started in the office and he still hasn't had a chance to become friends with her. Afsaneh is one of those girls who attract attention. He's heard she's from a rich, well-known family: the Afsharnia. Some people know them.

She ignores those following her with their eyes. Slithers away like a fish. Sussan acts as a go-between and invites them to a restaurant. She's witty and quick. Encouraged, he invites her to dine with him the next week. They go to a restaurant outside the city. He doesn't take his eyes off her the whole time they're together. He hasn't the nerve to ask her to marry him. He waits. The third time, he wants to take her to a restaurant in Darband. She refuses to go there. They go farther away. They talk about everything. Sometimes she's quiet, and he wonders what she is thinking about. She hasn't finished her food. Then he says he loves her. He can't finish his sentence. She's staring at him, liveliness and sadness in her eyes. He can't breathe. Afsaneh is quiet, too. He proposes to her. She smiles an answer: yes. He presses her hand. He has no courage to kiss her in front of people. His appetite returns. He orders a big dessert. Returning home, they are quiet. He can't believe she accepted his proposal. He's waiting for her to change her mind. He lets her off at her place. She invites him in. They enter the apartment, and their lips are on each other. When he regains control of himself, he has Afsaneh in his arms, they are lying together, naked. He trembles, thinking about what has happened. He can't believe Afsaneh yields herself so easily. He can't believe he is the first man in her life.

He looks at her. She's beautiful. Her big brown eyes shine in her wheat complexion. She's a goddess. Flawless.

"What we did wasn't right," he says.

"Why?"

"Because you and me, just today..."

She says, "You asked me to marry you and I accepted. Isn't that enough?"

"You mean no one ever asked you to marry?"

"Or if someone did, I didn't accept."

"But the wedding…"

She laughs loudly, wrapping his body in her arms, kissing him. She says, "This is the marriage, isn't it enough?"

He presses her to his chest. He has found a treasure, a valuable treasure.

The trees rustle. A cold breeze is blowing, it's starting to rain hard. He doesn't mind getting soaked. Perhaps the feeling of being drunk will leave him. No, he's not drunk. Alcohol has no affect on him, it makes him more conscious. His mind becomes more clear. The past won't leave him alone. He's soaked through to the bone. He goes inside the cabin, stands at the window, watching the rain. If Afsaneh was here. Afsaneh, she was a natural. Afsaneh taught him about nature. Taught him what she found in trees, in stars, in the sunset, in the sunrise. In nature, she became enchanted, intoxicated, generous, she read poetry, sang songs, intoxicated him, too. Afsaneh was a river, no, she was a mountain, a forest, she was earth, she was rain – saturating the earth, fertilizing it. She wanted to be fertile, but it didn't happen. She wanted it with all her heart, but he couldn't make her pregnant. Afsaneh left him, left... No she didn't leave him. She is here, somewhere among the trees, among the drops of rain or in the breeze, in that bird's song...

"Come over here and look. Look, how magnificent the mountains are."

The green, northern mountains spread out ahead of them. They were driving back from up north. Five days and nights in the water, in ecstasy. Afsaneh was happy. If she didn't talk about having children, he would be happy too. The first night she remembered her wish. Like a bindweed, she wrapped him in her arms, wanted a child from him. He didn't dare tell her that he couldn't give it to her. What happened to his courage? For a year he struggled with himself and didn't dare tell the truth. He should have told her the first day. He couldn't. Afsaneh put him in a difficult position. On this trip, she wanted to draw his sterilized being into herself.

Afsaneh is happy and full of desire. This morning, driving to

Tehran, she has been talking. She is animated again. She may leave him. She will leave him for certain. Her whole body yearns for a baby. She wants to revive her lost childhood through her own children. Her own children.

It's a year since they married and Afsaneh is restless. She's captivated by the mountains to the north – covered by trees and the silence of their valleys. A gentle wind is blowing. He's angry, stifled, doesn't know what to do. Afsaneh has taken all his courage. He feels like he's nothing compared to her. He doesn't want to feel worse than he does now. If Afsaneh knows why he can't have a baby, if she knows, she'll leave him.

He had a right to do it. He didn't want to be a hermit. He did it to punish himself. He didn't want any children. He didn't want to be a father. He couldn't manage it. If Afsaneh hadn't enchanted him, he would never have accepted the responsibility of having a wife and family. He never did. He didn't want to spoil the pleasure of having sex. He didn't want to. He didn't.

Afsaneh's voice brought him back to himself.

"What happened? Why are you so quiet."

He smiles. He wants to kiss her cheeks, but he avoids it. In front of people? It's not right. Her long gray dress with big padded shoulders covers her down to her toes. Her Balouchi scarf, with its vivid colours, which she bought up north, covers her hair. She looks different in this attire. This Afsaneh is different from who she is at home. She controls her laughter which pours from her like a waterfall; she hides her smile. Staring at him, she says, "What's the matter with you?"

"Nothing," he answers coldly.

"You know what I want to talk about."

"How would I know?"

"About a baby. I've made my decision."

He wants to laugh. He wants to laugh loudly. Laugh to forget about his fear, have courage and tell the truth.

"What?"

"If the problem is with you, if I were sure you couldn't have a baby, it's alright. We can adopt, one or two or even three children. We can, can't we? Financially, we can afford it. So many children are without parents since the war."

He doesn't hear the rest. He sits at a table. The waiter comes by and he orders tea. It's after ten in the morning. The weather in the mountains is cool. A gentle wind is blowing, bringing a nice chill from the tree-covered mountains, and the smell of the countryside. Afsaneh is still standing, watching the mountains. She walks toward him. The boy brings them two glasses of tea, with a dish of sugar cubes. Afsaneh looks more serious. He knows she's hurt because he isn't listening. She sits at the table quietly. He puts his hand on hers and looks into her eyes. To change the subject he says, "Fix your scarf properly. Your hair is out."

She arranges her scarf on her head, saying angrily, "Can't we even be free in the mountains?"

He looks at Afsaneh, smiling. He knows she hasn't forgotten the subject. As she opens her mouth to say something, he talks about the population problem, about insecurity in human societies, about violence, about bringing a human being into this world against its own will, just for ourselves. A big sin, a crime, he says.

Afsaneh looks at him, disbelieving. "What dark glasses you've put on."

"It's the world that's dark. I didn't make it that way."

The world is dark. It's raining and a cloud has covered the sky. The bench and tent are wet. The trees are shaking their leaves joyfully. They're probably hiding Afsaneh. The forest is quiet, abandoned to the rain washing it. What happened to the birds? Perhaps they've hidden and will come out after the rain. The squirrels and mosquitoes are gone too. What happened to Afsaneh? He saw her a few minutes ago, standing between two trees, as if taking a shower under the tree.

"She left me." He knew she would go. From the first day he met her, he knew she would leave. From the first time he took her in his arms, and wine flew through his veins, he knew she would flee. She was like a breeze, he couldn't keep her in his hand, she blew away. Even after she left, he still felt her presence. He still feels her, she's there, in the rain, watching.

"Why didn't you tell me earlier?"

"Earlier? When?"

"Before our marriage."

"I wanted to, but when we slept together, before marriage, I was obliged to marry you. You hadn't been with any other man..."

"Does that matter to you? Why was it just with me you were dutiful? What about the girl?"

"Well, I had a responsibility to you. I mean I felt I had to be responsible. I didn't want it to be the same..."

"Responsibility? What responsibility?"

"You understand."

"Why are you talking so mysteriously? I was an adult. I was twenty-eight. I wanted to sleep with you. Nobody forced me. I didn't ask you to marry me. I talked about having children from the first day. I told you how much I wanted children."

"Yes, you did."

"And you were silent. You didn't tell me you couldn't have a baby. You kept me waiting two years. Whenever I slept with you, I imagined I was pregnant. I was happy dreaming of being pregnant, and if my period was a day or two late, I was sure I was pregnant, and you... How many times did that happen? Do you remember? You saw me living happily in a dream and said nothing."

She should understand. Why didn't she understand? I had punished myself. She didn't want to understand. She left. Selfish!

The rain stops. It's humid inside the cabin. He opens the fridge door, another bottle of whiskey there.

"No, I don't want alcohol. I don't want to be drunk. Why should I get drunk? What help is being drunk?"

He's conscious. He has always been conscious. Alcohol makes him more conscious. But he's had enough. He takes a bunch of grapes from the fridge. He's not hungry, he's just empty. Alcohol has made him empty. His insides are empty, his head is empty, his whole existence is empty. Afsaneh has left him. No she hasn't. She's talking to him. Talking. Words accumulate in him. If she was there, he would talk to her for twenty-four hours, forty-eight hours, forever. Open his life completely to her. Why didn't he? For two years, he talked nonsense and absurdities.

Bahram leaves the cabin. The sky is clear. A few birds sing, celebrating the end of the rain. As if they are at a party. The sun is in the sky. The clouds are like happy guests leaving. No, they're wandering this way and that. They're happy. He's the only one who's not happy. He has left too much unsaid. The grape in his mouth is tasteless, acrid. He spits the seeds out. A squirrel appears from among the trees and comes close. The bench is wet. Bahram sits on the bench, and his clothes get wet. He feels cold inside and trembles. The sun is hot. He gets up and walks through the trees to the beach. The leaves shake, pouring raindrops on him. He's waiting for Afsaneh. She's somewhere around. Or inside him. Yes, Afsaneh is with him. She never left him. She pulls him to her.

The lake stretches under the sun. It seems joyful and happy. Why shouldn't it be? It has Afsaneh. For a year, Afsaneh has been sleeping in the lake's arms. It should be happy. The joy of sleeping with Afsaneh...

Negar was wrong. She didn't move somewhere else, she's here, in this lake, in this forest, among these trees. I know how much she loves to be with nature. I know for sure.

A few people are in the water. They've been waiting for the sun to come out, to throw themselves into the arms of the lake.

It's warm and humid. Bahram sits on a rock. The sun has slid to the west, it's the middle of the afternoon. Clouds gather on the horizon. One white cloud has paused like a boat in the middle of the sky. There are sailboats on the lake. The natural world and the people are happy; Bahram is like a ball of sorrow. He yearns to be one with this rock, to become stone. The seagulls are happy too. Why are they screaming? They fly down to the surface of the water and soar up. A few children are imitating the seagulls' cry. The sky shelters them all. He looks at his watch, reads it and then forgets what time is. Angrily, he tosses his watch into the lake. Get rid of time. Freedom! Yes, he should free himself. He looks at the water, it can give him refuge. The lake is like a mother, like his mother, opening her arms to him. The lake holds Afsaneh in its arms. The lake at night.

His breath is heavy. Is it so easy? Is it enough to decide to die? Yes, it is. He doesn't want to let his breath out. He keeps his breath in. Death...

"Come on, don't be afraid."

He's watching Behnaz. The families have left the beach and are sitting on the balcony of the villa. It's late afternoon and the sky is cloudy. Fereshteh is standing by the beach, watching Bahram and Behnaz. She's wearing her black swimming suit and has a towel on her shoulders. She trembles in the cold wind. Mother and Father, Behjat and her husband are all on the balcony of the villa facing the sea. The wind carries their voices. Fereshteh tells them, "Come out, it's cold and the sea is getting rough."

Behnaz, at a distance from him, is sitting in the water, her swimming suit is bright. Her short hair is stuck to her head, her face is pale with cold. She stretches her arms towards Fereshteh, calling, "Just two more minutes."

Fereshteh says, "I'm going to dress but in two minutes I'll be back and both of you must be out of the water and going to the villa." Bahram tosses a handful of sand at Behnaz. The sand disperses in the water. That's a high wave coming towards shore. Behnaz's back is to the wave. She throws herself into the water, screaming, "Look, I can lie on the water."

The wave is coming closer in a rush. He must yell, be careful Behnaz. Behnaz is floating on the water, shaking her hands and legs. Behnaz is courageous. Father says she should be a boy. The white foam of the wave closes in on Behnaz like a monster. Bahram turns and runs to the shore. The wave catches his feet. He stays on shore and waits for Behnaz. She has disappeared. There's no sign of her bright swimsuit on the sea. He doubts she went to the villa. He goes to the villa, meets Fereshteh still in her swimming suit, leaning on the fence. She asks him, "What about Behnaz?"

He shakes his head, he doesn't know. Fereshteh runs to the sea, screaming, "Behnaz."

Mother and Father, Behjat and Mr. Refahi, also run to the shore. The sea is restless. Wave after wave hits the shore. Now Bahram understands. The wave has taken Behnaz out to the sea. The scream jams in his throat.

His mother takes him in her arms, saying, "My son isn't guilty."

Father slapped his face, screaming, "Stupid boy, tell me what happened? Did you drown the child?"

His tongue is frozen, he simply screams.

The lighthouse is glimmering far away. Waves pound the shore angrily.

The next morning, Behnaz's body is retrieved from the sea and is buried in a cemetery close to the sea. Father is cold to him for a long time. Bahram hides in his mother's arms and has nightmares.

"I was only nine and Behnaz was seven and half. I didn't love her. She competed with me in everything. She was better than me at everything, school and games. But I didn't want to drown her. That day I wanted to scream, a wave was getting close, but my tongue froze. I couldn't control it."

"And now do you feel guilty?"

"Aren't I guilty?"

"Sometimes it's not possible to avoid an accident."

They are sitting on the balcony of Majid Khan's villa. Afsaneh wants to stay overnight, Bahram says, no, he can't. Afsaneh asks, why, and he tells her about Behnaz. For the first time in his life he describes the event as it happened. Afsaneh sympathizes with him, they return to the hotel to sleep.

"Later on we never went to the villa, or to the north. My Father sold the villa."

"Because of that you're afraid of the sea?"

"Afraid? No, the memory hurts."

"But you were only nine."

"It's true, but even then, sometimes evil thoughts came to me. That something should happen to Behnaz. That day the same thought crossed my mind. But it was only a thought."

"Those thoughts aren't strange for a nine-year-old child."

"But her drowning made me happy. Those hysterical screams were of joy, I thought, joy or shock. Well, then I had nightmares. Nightmares about the sea, about being drowned. They took me to a psychologist and he made me believe I wasn't guilty."

"And you accepted that?"

"I had to, to get rid of those nightmares. I forced myself to believe I wasn't guilty. Behnaz pestered me for no reason. She envied me. I liked being friends with her, she was very smart. She was better than me at everything, even at telling big lies."

Afsaneh laughs loudly.

"Even at telling lies she was better than you?"

"Yes, she was a strange one. She was trying for our parents. Especially my mother. My father loved her. He always used to say, I wish Behnaz was a boy and you were a girl. He believed I was like a girl, timid and clumsy. But Behnaz was brave, fearless. She had a special place in my father's heart. But she got on my mother's nerves. Mother was kinder to me than to Behnaz. She always gave the best food to me. I was a nine-year-old and still slept in my mother's bed. Behnaz slept in Fereshteh's bed."

"Didn't you have your own bed?"

"No, I don't remember having a separate bed as a child. When I got older they gave me a single bed. When Fereshteh married, the children's room was mine. I was fourteen."

"You mean until fourteen, you slept in your mother's bed? And if your father wanted to…"

"My father had a separate bedroom. Later on, I heard it was after Behnaz's birth that my father got his bedroom. He sent Mother to the children's room."

"To sleep in your arms?"

Her loud laugh hurts him.

Afsaneh looks at him. Her eyes are full of hate and humiliation. He feels himself changing into a worm, that Afsaneh will step on him and crush him.

"The day you talked about your sister who was drowned and the guilt you felt, why did you forget about Hanna? Why didn't you tell me that you forced the poor girl to kill herself? Had you justified it to yourself and didn't need to talk about it?"

He doesn't answer. Why can't he talk about Hanna? If he talked about her, would she still be with him? Afsaneh is forcing him to confess. He has punished himself for his sin. He has paid for his misbehaviour.

The doctor is a man from East Asia. His accent is Vietnamese or Chinese. He stares at Bahram with his narrow eyes.

"Are you sure you've made the correct decision?"

"Yes," Bahram says coldly.

He wants to do it before he changes his mind. It's six months since Hanna's death, and in these six months, he hasn't dared have sex with a woman.

Violet, a classmate says, "Maybe you have a problem."

He says, "I'm afraid you'll get pregnant."

She says, "I take the pill."

He doesn't believe her.

She says, "If you don't believe me, use protection."

He can't. Violet makes fun of him. Diana too. And he's restless. He wants a woman badly. He takes a woman from the street to his place, and is unable to get aroused. The woman looks at him with disdain, "If you're afraid, get sterilized."

Her words stay with him. He should do it. "So I won't have any offspring."

"My dear boy, to be a father is to accept responsibilities." He doesn't want responsibilities.

"Do you have a special reason that you don't want to have children?"

Reason? He looks for a reason. Hanna. Yes, he has a reason. But he can't talk about it to the doctor.

"I want to marry," he says.

The doctor's eyes widen a little.

"Well, that seems odd. You want to marry and you're making this decision? What does your fiancée say?"

"It's her decision. Her health isn't good enough to have a baby and I ..."

"This is a great sacrifice."

Afsaneh is sitting far away. He wants to put his head on her shoulders. He wants Afsaneh to take him in her arms. Like the day he talked about Behnaz drowning, and she said, "It's best to forget it. You can't relive the past." Today, there's no sympathy in her eyes.

"Do you feel guilty?"

"Before I sterilized myself, I felt guilty, but after..."

"After, you could sleep with any woman you liked and forget about it."

"Afsaneh," he says, "I was only twenty. My father forced me to do it, I didn't want to."

"And you, like a nine-year-old boy, ineffectual and naïve, submitted yourself to your father's will. Maybe you laughed inside. One of those hysteric laughs that make others suspicious. About to be a father, and you let your father make a decision to abandon that innocent girl?"

Afsaneh frowns at him. He's silent. Afsaneh's look is full of disapproval. "I can't believe you," she says, "you wanted it to happen like that. Just like you wished Behnaz to drown, you also wanted something to happen to Hanna, you wanted to get rid of Hanna, too. She got pregnant and you didn't know how to get rid of it. Why did you call your father? Did you want him to recite your wedding vows for you? I know why you brought your father here. You wanted to place the guilt on his shoulders, instead of yours. Why, when you made love with Hanna, didn't you ask your father's permission?"

He has a flight tomorrow. The whole family is at their house. It's a farewell party. Father calls him to his bedroom, the room his father has slept in alone since Behnaz's birth. No longer his mother's room. Father doesn't want more daughters. Four daughters and one son.

Bahram sits on a chair. His father is sitting by his desk. The room is tidy and clean. The curtains are pulled aside and behind the window is the big yard with lamps lit. It is the first month of summer and the garden is full of plants and flowers. Behjat's and Fereshteh's children are playing in the yard. Nargess has called from Belgium and asked Bahram's father to buy a ticket to Canada through Belgium so Bahram can stay a few days with them and her sons could meet their uncle.

The father says, "Well, my son, you're a man now. From now on, you stand on your own feet. You won't have your mother and Nanny Afagh with you anymore to tidy your bed, wash your clothes, and serve your food. Your father won't be there either, to tell you what to do and what not to do. You're in charge of your own life. Over there, study hard, and take advantage of the possibilities first. And then, if you like, you can enjoy your life. A man should be able to enjoy his own youth. You can be with your female class-mates. A man should have experience before marriage. Of course after marriage, too, there's no restriction. Otherwise life loses its flavour. You shouldn't enjoy only one type of fruit your whole life. You'll get sick of it. Each flower has its own perfume. Thank God you're not a girl, or I would have to advise you to be careful about your virginity."

His father's look is cold. He's sitting on the only chair, re-proach in his eyes. The day before, Hanna swept the room and tidied it. Bahram has taken Hanna's photo off his desk. He didn't dare show it to his father, before meeting her. They've returned from the restaurant. All the way from the restaurant to the apart-ment, his father hasn't uttered one word. It's as if Bahram is a child who has done something wrong. Bahram doesn't dare open his mouth. He's afraid that if he says something, his father will get angry, and yell at him, as he did in Iran. His father plays with his beads, ignoring him. Bahram sits on his bed, and watches his fa-ther warily. Their eyes meet for a moment.

"My dear boy, if I had a baby with all the women I slept with, half of Tehran's population would be your brothers and sisters. You know it's been years since I touched your mother, since the birth of my poor Behnaz. Do you think I was a hermit all these years? No, my son. A man needs a bedmate, just like he needs food, or air. Do you remember that I told you to enjoy your life? I didn't want you to be an ascetic and not make any mistakes. But I didn't tell you to be so clumsy. Didn't you know, if you sleep with a woman she might become pregnant? And a modest girl like that, Black..."

His father's words make him angry, and he notices it. His voice gets louder, "You should get rid of her. It's your family or her, choose one."

When Bahram enters the restaurant, Hanna is sitting by a table. Her belly isn't visible under her loose coat. She smiles at him. He sits in front of her, without removing his coat. It's raining outside. He asks, "Would you like to eat something?"

She nods no, with her smile. Her eyes are talking to him, looking at him in silence. He realizes she has understood everything from his face. He doesn't know how to begin. Hanna is like a stranger to him. He sees the reflection of his father's derision on her face. He hears his father's voice. "You should get rid of her."

Hanna's voice distracts his thoughts.

"Well, what did your father say?"

"We have to separate for a while," he says.

Hanna's big eyes are full of sadness. Staring at him, she stays quiet.

"Just for a while. After my father leaves, we can be together again."

"When does he leave?" she asks.

"I don't know, he wants to buy an apartment for me."

"My baby will be born in four months."

He looks out the window. Your mother wants a blue-eyed grandchild and you...

Rain hits the window. Cars, different models and colours, are parked on the street, washed by the rain. He slides the envelope toward her.

"What's this?" she asks.

"Open it."

She opens the envelope with hesitation. Her smile fades. Sadness covers her face. Her silence bothers him. He has never seen Hanna so quiet and withdrawn. He expected her to be happy to see the cheque. Instead, there's indignation on her face. Then, "For what?"

"It's from my father."

She shoves the cheque into the envelope and flings it at him. They stare at each other. He sees humiliation in Hanna's eyes. He is wet with sweat. Hanna pushes her chair aside angrily, gets up. She doesn't look at him. She leaves the restaurant, and is lost among the cars, in the street.

They moved to the new apartment. He bought it before Afsaneh arrived in Montreal. Afsaneh is fervent, as she was at the beginning of their marriage. All day she wanders through stores, sometimes she calls him at his job. She wants to know what he thinks about something she'd like to purchase for their apartment. He has left it to her to choose what she wants. The apartment faces the St. Lawrence River. She asked him just once where the money came from. He answered that when he was a student, his father had bought him a small apartment, which he sold for the down payment on this one. Afsaneh brought her green rug from Iran. The rug is old and doesn't match their other furniture.

"Afsaneh, could you spread your treasure somewhere else?" he says sarcastically.

"This is my only remembrance of my parents," she says, "I wouldn't change this rug for anything in the world. The green reminds me of Ozra's and Firoozeh's eyes."

He has to accept it. He's glad Afsaneh has come to Canada. He takes her to a restaurant every night. They finish a bottle of wine, walk in the empty streets. He's grown to love Afsaneh more. Something in her dazzles, charms him. When he takes her in his arms, his lips on hers, he's afraid she'll melt or evaporate into the sky. He's waiting for her to talk about having a baby. He has decided to tell her the truth. She has to accept it. The truth. How will he tell it, so that she believes it? The truth. He doesn't know what the truth is.

Afsaneh is lying down on a sofa, apparently daydreaming. Soft music is playing. She has a book in her hand. It's evening and a breeze is blowing in from the river. The sky is cloudy, the air smells of rain. Bahram worries about Afsaneh's silence. He guesses what she's thinking, and worries. His guess is correct. "A house without children, is sad," Afsaneh says, "even if all its furniture is beautiful and there's music, it's still lifeless. Something is missing."

He wants to say, do you want to have the same conversation again? She stares at him, perceiving another side of him.

"Why haven't you told me you had a child in Canada?" Her eyes fix on him. He reddens, and his entire body flushes with sweat, like a person caught stealing. He wishes the earth would open up and swallow him. She asks firmly, "Why haven't you told me?"

Bahram doesn't answer. He goes out onto the balcony. The whole city is visible. The river seems motionless. The sun is hidden behind a heap of clouds. Afsaneh sits on the sofa. He looks at her. She is bent, her head in her hands. He goes to her, sits on the floor beside her. He takes her hands in his and asks, "How did you find out?"

"Sussan told me," she says. Looking into his eyes, she asks again, "Why didn't you tell me?"

"It was hard to talk about," he says.

"What do you mean?"

"It was a mistake. I was only twenty. I didn't have any experience."

Her face lights up with joy. "So, you can have a baby?"

He doesn't answer her. He closes her mouth with a long kiss. The same Afsaneh she was at the beginning of their marriage. Full of desire. She goes to a specialist; the doctors assure her she has no problems. She wants a baby from him. Each time she sleeps with him, she repeats, "I've decided to get pregnant. It's late. I'm already thirty years old. I don't want my children to have an old mother, like my grandmother. No, my children won't want a grandmother."

She's happy she's come to Canada. The apartment is full of

music. She laughs, she sings; during her period, she's restless. Her eyes are full of expectation and energy. Her body is burning up, but when she wants to talk about the baby in her womb, he refuses to listen. He can't look her in the eyes. And again she becomes quiet. She has her monthly cramps. She blames herself, and cries. Hugging him, begging him to give her a baby, she says, "I want to find my lost childhood in my own children."

He presses her to his chest, and doesn't dare tell her the truth. He's afraid. Afraid she will leave him. Afsaneh is only staying with him to get pregnant. If she knows, what would she do?

Bahram goes to Negar's. She opens the door for him. He can't believe she's Ramin's wife. He's never seen a picture of her. He has found her telephone number through the Iranian community in Toronto. He wants to help her. He's heard she's not a coping woman. He has to help her. Afsaneh is with him day and night like a devil. She nags him. Afsaneh and Hanna won't leave him alone. They are his nightmares. Every night he takes a different woman back to his home, but nothing changes. Afsaneh and Hanna are with him all the time. He doesn't know what to do. He thinks if he helps Negar, he might have peace. He calls her, and introduces himself. She's quiet, surprised. Bahram doesn't know what Afsaneh has said about him.

"Afsaneh never spoke about you."

"Never?"

"Never. I've only heard your name."

"What picture did you have of me?"

"None."

Her young face reddens with discomfort and embarrassment. Her eyes are gray. Her hair, dishevelled, reaches her shoulders. Her beauty is childish and charming, her voice hesitant. She has white hands with tiny fingers, and wears a wedding ring. Her little boy is like herself, he appears naïve and vulnerable. He doesn't take his eyes off Bahram. He would hurt quickly, and cry easily.

Getting along with Negar and her son would be difficult, Bahram thinks. On his second visit, he takes an expensive toy for Damon, and invites Negar to a restaurant. She doesn't want to go.

"What would people say about me?"

"People? What people? What do you care? Are you going to tell everyone that you want to go out to dinner with me?"

"But my friends know everything about my life."

"Your friends? Which friends?"

"Mehdi, Mahboobeh. They're very kind to me. I mean, since Ramin left."

"Left?"

"Left with Afsaneh. You know about them."

"Are you sure he's gone? The newspaper said they probably drowned. I'm certain they've drowned."

"But their bodies haven't been found."

"They will be found."

"And some people say they moved to somewhere, Australia or South America perhaps. If they did, Ramin will come back. I know he'll be back. I know how much he loves Damon."

"And if he comes, will you take him back?"

Negar looks amazed. There's uncertainty in her gray eyes. As if she can't believe what has happened. During the week, he calls her several times. She agrees to dinner with him. He goes to her place. She's hardly wearing any make-up. Her eyes are green now, her hair blond. She looks prettier and younger. He's brought a dress for her from Montreal. She opens the wrapping paper, and like a child, can't hide her joy. She moves to kiss him, then stops. He hugs her and plants a kiss on her forehead. She's tiny and fragile; light as a cloud. Her little boy is standing by, watching them. He's happy too, busy with his new toy, a remote-controlled car. Bahram shows him how to make it move.

Over dinner in the restaurant, he nods at her to talk. She re-tells her life, her childhood, Ramin. She talks less about Afsaneh.

Negar doesn't like to speak about her. She hates her and can't hide her hatred. She sees the anger in Bahram's face, and stops talking. Negar acts vulnerable and defenseless. She says clearly she can't live without help.

Bahram gives her a ride home, kisses her. Her little boy is sleeping on the back seat. Negar wants to wake him up. Bahram doesn't let her. He lifts him up and carries him into the apartment, barely taking his eyes off Negar. She slides her eyes away shyly. He puts the child to bed, takes Negar in his arm and kisses her. Bahram wants to sleep with her. But she doesn't want to, and starts to cry.

"Why?"

"No, I can't."

"Maybe you're not ready."

She extracts herself from his arms and goes to the washroom. He waits a while and then knocks at the door. Negar comes out. Bahram says goodbye to her and leaves. He has made his decision. He must come to Toronto or take them to Montreal. Since he took Negar and her child under his wing, Afsaneh and Hanna bother him less. No other woman is of any interest to him. He talks to her during the week, lets her talk about her life and her feelings. She talks about her hostility toward Afsaneh. He's happy. His life has acquired meaning. Whenever he goes to see Negar and Damon, he brings gifts for them, and takes them to the suburbs to eat in expensive restaurants. He sees appreciation and joy in their faces. He admires Negar's beauty. He talks about his decision and she can't believe it. When he says, "I'm serious," she opens her arms to him. She wears a ring he brought from Montreal, and they celebrate at a restaurant. He orders expensive wine. Negar doesn't want to drink more than half a glass, but that half makes her feel drunk. Her cheeks are red. He goes to her place and sleeps with her. He wants to undress her, but she refuses. Perhaps Ramin is still in her mind, perhaps she is still waiting for him. But she has agreed to live with him. He will sell his apartment in Montreal and buy a house in Toronto. She wants a house with a backyard where her little boy can play. In summer, she plans to put in a swing, white chairs on a deck and a barbecue.

Two weeks later, Bahram returns to Toronto unexpectedly. It's mid-week. A real estate agent wants to show him a house in Richmond Hill which is a good deal. He goes to Negar's place. Damon opens the door for him. Negar is in the bathroom, taking a shower. He opens the bathroom door, watches her for a while behind the shower curtain. She looks like a formless ghost, caressing her belly, and he notices that her belly is swollen. It seems big for her body. He closes the bathroom door quietly. She's pregnant. His heart sinks.

Afsaneh kisses him saying, "The doctor says, there's no problem with me. It's your turn to see a doctor. It might be you."

Bahram wants to say, I'm sterilized. He doesn't.

The child isn't mine. Is she going to bed with others too, he wonders.

He sits on the sofa and waits for Negar to come out of the bathroom. He says to Damon, "Tell her that I'm here and to hurry up."

When she sees him, she is surprised and screams. She puts her hand on her belly involuntarily.

"Sit down," he says coldly.

She sits uncertainly in a corner of the sofa. He speaks formally.

"Why didn't you tell me?" he asks.

"What?" she asks, puzzled.

He nods at her belly. She starts to cry.

"You should be truthful with me," he says coldly, "I can't stand hollering and crying."

"Ramin left me because of this baby. Ramin didn't want to have children. Because I became pregnant, he left with Afsaneh."

He hugs her and says, "But I like the idea. We'll celebrate tonight for this baby. I want it to be a girl. I'll call her Afsaneh."

They view the house he's going to buy. Negar is delighted. They go on to a restaurant. Bahram stays overnight and she sleeps in his arms, naked. He's happy Negar is pregnant. He convinces himself the baby is his. He wants the baby to be a girl, so he'll have a complete family, a girl and a boy. He talks to Afsaneh in his mind, telling her, what you yearned and wished for, I got. They fell from the sky for me. He feels relaxed for the first time. At night he dreams about Afsaneh. He's washing Damon in the tub, telling Afsaneh, "Look, what a handsome boy I have."

Damon is sitting in a full tub.

Afsaneh says, "He's not your son, he's mine. I got pregnant by Ramin and gave birth to him. You're sterilized. You can't have a baby. Damon is my son. I love him more than my life. I gave him life."

Bahram becomes angry and shoves Damon's head under the water, holding it there until he drowns. Damon is lying on his back in the water. Afsaneh looks at Bahram with revulsion, "Killer, killer," she screams.

Bahram wakes. Negar is crumpled in the corner of the bed, naked. He covers her with the sheet, leaves the bed. He sits on the sofa in the living room. The roses he brought yesterday for Negar have died. Their stems are bent. He is still in the dream. "Killer." He feels like a stranger in his surroundings. He asks himself, am I doing the right thing? I don't love them. Then he dismisses his thought. They are the only things that calm him.

A young girl steps out of the lake. She's the same height as Hanna. Her skin is the colour of brown brick, her wet hair shines in the sunlight. She is wearing a red bikini, perfect against her skin. She stands with her back to him. He stares at her body. Hanna lies on a bed. A white sheet covers her body. A policeman pulls the sheet aside. He wants to hold her face in his hands, tell her, "Hanna, wake up, it's me" and have her answer, "Baram," as she calls him, laughing with her whole face.

Her white teeth remind him of a pearl necklace his father brought for his mother from Macao. Whenever his mother wore it, she used to say, "I'll keep it for your wife."

The girl turns back and looks at him. Her resemblance to Hanna shocks him. He blinks several times to be sure he's not dreaming. The girl says something about the sky, the scattered white clouds. He hears the girl's voice but her words aren't clear. A lump sticks in his throat. The girl walks a few steps toward him, "The weather is wonderful," she says.

He gets up and hurries into the trees. Quickly, Hanna might be following. He turns back. The girl's face and Hanna's occupy his mind. He can't remember Hanna clearly, just her white teeth when she laughed joyfully. Her laughter whispers among the leaves. He stops walking and listens. "Am I crazy?" He walks through the trees along a path back to the lake. Here, the beach is rocky and empty. Seagulls scream over the lake, down to the surface of water, rise again to the blue sky. A mosquito buzzes near his ear, Bahram feels its sting on his neck. He scratches. He stands on a rock and watches the lake. There's a sailboat far out on the lake. Hanna, and the girl, have disappeared. Inside him, someone cries, "Crazy!"

Afsaneh sits in front of him. She's been in Montreal more than three months. Last night, they talked again about having children. She knows he had a child years ago. She wants to know why he doesn't want to have any more children. He tells her again, he's not ready yet. In veiled words, she tells him that's she's sorry she's come to Canada. He hasn't convinced her. When she stares at him, he feels intimidated. He knows she could draw the truth from him. Afsaneh doubts him, she understands that something is being hidden from her. Sometimes he reddens involuntarily when Afsaneh stares at him. Afsaneh becomes suspicious. "What's the matter with you? You're not being truthful with me."

He ignores her, looks at his plate of food.

"Why don't you answer me?"

"Will you let me eat my food?"

She falls quiet. She hasn't touched her food. He asks how she has spent her day. Afsaneh doesn't answer. "Why are you angry?" he asks.

Afsaneh stares at him. He feels she knows everything from his eyes. He blushes.

"Why shouldn't I be angry?" Afsaneh says, "Monotony! Silence! Why can't you understand? Tell me, what are you hiding from me? Why didn't you tell me that you had a child?"

He pushes his food aside, half-eaten. Getting up, he goes onto the balcony. A cold wind is blowing. He says to himself, "Tell her everything, be finished with it." He curses himself, enraged at his own cowardliness. He can't bear the cold wind, and returns to the living room. Afsaneh has taken the dinner dishes to the kitchen. He hugs her, takes her to the living room. He seats her on a sofa, begins kissing her. He wants to sleep with her. Afsaneh pushes him away saying, "What's the use?"

"Must making love have a use?"

"Leave me alone," she says impatiently.

He looks at her eyes, her disappointment. Her suspicion brings him to tears. Afsaneh is worried about him. "What happened?"

"Nothing," he says, wiping the tears.

"Talk to me," she says coldly and authoritatively, "I can't stand this kind of life any longer."

Gazing into Afsaneh's eyes, he feels pity for her. He has deceived her, and she doesn't know she's deceived. He suddenly understands he's making another mistake. He can't hide his secret any more.

"I can't have children."

"Haven't you before?"

"Yes, but I can't anymore."

She stares at him shocked, "Why?"

"I had myself sterilized."

Afsaneh doesn't believe him. He sees it in her eyes. She doesn't believe him.

"Don't lie to me."

He expects Afsaneh to believe him. He thinks about taking back his own words. He's looking for another reason, but he can't find one. Afsaneh's suspicious eyes paralyze him. She says with the same commanding tone of voice, "Why are you hiding the truth from me?"

"Believe me. I was sterilized. I can't have children anymore."

"Why? Were you sick?" she asks, still suspicious.

"It's a long story."

"Long? Tell me the whole story."

Afsaneh's look changed. She moves away from him as he explains. He finishes a half-full bottle of whiskey in the course of telling everything as it happened. She pulls farther away. The smell of alcohol bothers her. When he finishes his story, Afsaneh gets up and goes to the balcony. Bahram is still sitting on the floor. He sees Afsaneh standing with her back to him. Beyond her is the cloudy October sky. The city lights glitter. A heavy silence dominates the apartment. He goes to the balcony and hugs Afsaneh, puts his head on her shoulders. She caresses his hair, carelessly. Her caress doesn't move him. His heart is empty.

Clouds cover the sun. Bahram hears voices, but it's not clear whether the sound is coming from among the trees or by the lake. He walks without knowing where he's going. He's restless. His heart is empty. He doesn't know what time it is. He doesn't have his watch. He tossed it into the lake, but he still checks his wrist.

He wanted to get rid of time. It hasn't freed him. Time passes, taking him with it. Where? He doesn't know. He wants to fuse with nature like Afsaneh could.

They're sitting at a table in the hotel facing the Caspian Sea. The sea is stormy. Afsaneh is watching the sea from the hotel restaurant. Her face, framed by her white scarf, looks pale. Her bright eyes are full of longing. They were awake very late last night. Sleeping with Afsaneh is exceptional, different from all his experiences, something beyond being one with her body. She's generous as the day, full of mysteries as the night. When he embraces her, she becomes even more mysterious. She rarely talks about herself. As if she didn't have a past. She lets him talk. He's told her everything about his life, except about Hanna. She listened to Behnaz's story with patience and consoled him by telling him he wasn't guilty. He wishes he could speak about Hanna too, wishes he could say he's sterilized, to stop her talking so much about the babies she will never have. But no, he leaves it for another time. He doesn't want to ruin the image she has of him.

Afsaneh watches the sea in silence. She's stopped talking, but she'll start again. She has a fire in her. Every movement, each development, stimulates her to talk. He enjoys her talk. He likes it when she speaks and he listens. When she's quiet, something nags him to speak, and he's afraid of speaking. Something reminds him of Hanna, and he wants to talk about her. No, he shouldn't mention her. He should forget her. Yes, forget. It was years ago.

"Why are you so quiet?" he asks.

Afsaneh turns back from the sea. He sees sadness in her eyes. For the first time, he notices the shadow of sadness and tears in her eyes. He wants to kiss her, then remembers they're in the restaurant. He presses her hands. Holds her long fingers in his.

"I was remembering being young."

"Your childhood? You've never talked about your childhood."

"I didn't have any childhood."

"What do you mean? Is it possible someone didn't have a childhood? You haven't always been this height and size."

She smiles. Her face is animated. Her smile is like a gentle breeze.

"No, I haven't always been this height and size. But I didn't have a childhood. My parents died very early."

"Why don't you talk about your childhood?"

"I don't have anything to say."

"Tell me about your youth."

She stares at the sea.

"Have you ever been in love?" he asks.

"Love?" she mumbles. After a pause, she recites a poem by Hafiz: "More pleasant than the sound of love's speech, naught I heard. A keepsake that, in this revolving dome remained."

He eyes her in silence. Sadness shadows her face. And again she recites. "Not pleasant than the sound of love's speech naught I heard. Oh Saki! Give wine, make short this hearing and uttering."

The waiter brings their food. At the plate of rice and fish, Afsaneh's face fills with delight.

Sunset shadows the lake. Returning along the path, Bahram smells a barbecue. The mosquitoes are more plentiful, stinging him. Night is on its way. It's windy, hunger squeezes his stomach. Thinking about food, he loses his appetite. He doesn't want to eat. Bahram wants to walk, to walk somewhere, but he doesn't know where. He likes the night and wants to get lost in the darkness, like a small stone.

He remembers Negar. He's surprised to have forgotten her for a while. He doesn't know for how long. He's glad she has left him. She has disappeared from his life. Good. He has to end that charade. He's finished with it.

Bahram has bought a house in Richmond Hill. He takes Negar to see the house. She's amazed and delighted. She can't believe it. Like a child receiving an unexpected toy, she's happy, bouncing up and down. After seeing the house he takes her to a restaurant. She wants to show her appreciation.

"I can't believe it," she says, "why are you so nice to me?"

She expects him to tell her he loves her, but he says, "You don't owe me anything. I'm doing it for myself." He sees the amazement in her eyes.

"I don't understand."

"I have a commitment I must fulfill."

She's confused. He likes her surprise, her simplicity, her excitement. She is like a puppet. He can make her move and dance. He's happy with her happiness.

"Do you feel a responsibility for me?" she asks. "You didn't force Ramin to leave me. And Afsaneh left you two years ago. You didn't force her to leave you."

"I might have."

She smiles. He likes to watch her — so simple, so naïve, so thankful.

"I was in love with Afsaneh," he says, "I still love her. Maybe one day I will go look for her."

There's fear in her eyes. She says, "But you said Afsaneh drowned."

"How can I be sure? You said they might have moved to Australia. Have you forgotten?"

"But they didn't come back. Nobody has heard about them since then."

"Are you still waiting for Ramin to come back?"

She doesn't answer, but with her eyes she says no. She's not waiting for him.

Bahram is in the canoe, paddling on the lake. The sky is clear, without a single cloud. A full moon shines brightly. Afsaneh is sitting beside him. She dissolves in the moonlight, the moon and Afsaneh became one. Afsaneh always became melancholy in moonlight. As if her genies surrounded her and led her away. And now, if she was here, she'd be in the middle of the lake, dancing in the darkness with her genies.

"Come on. Don't be frightened. Nights and days are the same in the sea. In any water. There isn't any sunlight, but the moon is here. The moon is more beautiful. Look."

Afsaneh is in the water. The sea is calm. The waves lick the shore, close to him, and die away.

"Don't be a child, Afsaneh," he says, "the sea here isn't safe. Who swims at night in the sea?"

She laughs loudly.

"Chicken. Don't do something that will make me call you chicken forever."

They've come to Ramsar for their honeymoon. He doesn't like Ramsar. He doesn't like the sea. The sea reminds him of Behnaz, makes him remember her. He hasn't mentioned it to Afsaneh. He knows how much she likes the sea. She says, "None of nature's manifestations are as mysterious as the sea. Only water can reflect everything in itself. It can give and receive life. The water is beautiful, frightening, and mysterious."

He talks about his childhood, when he saw the reflection of the moon in their pond and imagined another moon in the depths of the earth. He says water has an attraction for him and he's afraid. Afsaneh convinces him to ignore his fear.

"The beaches aren't safe here," he says.

She laughs and says, "Maybe you don't have confidence in yourself. The sea isn't rough. You know how to swim. What are you afraid of?"

Afsaneh floats on the water; Bahram stands on the shore. A wave passes over Afsaneh and before he can run away, the wave has reached him, wetting his shoes and pant legs. Afsaneh stands up. Watching him move farther away, she says, "If you don't come, I'll be gone."

She throws herself into the water and swims away. He takes his clothes off, leaves them beside Afsaneh's and enters the sea. The water reaches his chest. It's cold. He wants to go back.

"Why are you going back?" she cries.

"It's cold, very cold," he says.

"Come over here, it's warmer here. If you swim you'll get warm."

She swims away. He dismisses his fear and follows her, swimming. He wants to stop, there's no ground under his feet. He trembles with fear, calling Afsaneh. His head is out of the water. Afsaneh swims back, asking, "What is it? Are you going back?"

"I want to, but I can't."

They swim toward shore, until they feel the ground under their feet. He feels safe. Afsaneh's face looks unfamiliar in the moonlight. Her eyes glitter, she's more beautiful, but something in her scares him. Her black shirt is pulled tight to her body, her teeth gleam, she seems like a fantasy. She looks up at the sky. "It's magnificent. This night won't be repeated. We have to remember it."

He hugs her, scared. She frees herself and swims away under water. He wants to follow her, but loses track of her direction. Farther out, there's no ground under his feet. Swimming back, he stands up, looking around. There's only water, the moon, and the sound of waves, scaring him. An animal cry bursts from his throat. He calls Afsaneh loudly. There's no answer. He feels death close by. Bahram swims a few meters, but can't continue. His legs and arms are numb. He feels death grasping his throat. Standing, he waits, trembling with fear. Behnaz is mocking him, calling him a chicken. The water splashes his face, he swallows mouthfuls of a salty water. He wants to swim to the shore, but doesn't see it. No light to show the direction. There's only the moon, watching him indifferently. He sees Behnaz's tiny body stretching on the water, a big wave rolling towards her. He trembles with fear, looks around for Afsaneh. She is lost in the black water like a genie.

"I know the genies. When I was a child, my playmates were genies. I see them sometimes. I see them in darkness."

Stretching his hands out on both sides he takes a few steps, and again there's nothing under his feet. He swims madly in the opposite direction and feels ground. He stands up and screams, "Afsaneh."

Two hands close his eyes. His whole body trembles, imagining the genies have captured him. His tongue is frozen. He hears Afsaneh's loud laughter, and can't believe it's her. He wraps his arms around her body. A lamp shimmers far away. His heart is still throbbing. He can't speak. Afsaneh talks and laughs non-stop. When the water is below their chests, they pause.

"I almost had a stroke," he says.

"Chicken."

He has her hand tightly in his, doesn't let her separate from him.

"Let's go back," he says.

She understands his fear is real.

"OK, we'll go back, but you will be sorry. Tomorrow night the sea may be rough."

Reaching shore, they dress and he wants to return to the hotel.

"Why hurry?" she says, "are you afraid of the beach, too?"

"Yes, I am. You should know."

"Okay. But a night like this won't happen again."

It didn't. Not for him. But it could tonight. Perhaps Afsaneh will raise her head out of the water and say, "Come on. Don't be afraid. Don't make me call you a chicken forever." And Bahram will dive into the water and go with her, together, to the bottom. To the feast of the sea fairies and the pond mother.

Afsaneh sets the food on the table, and sits at the other end. She's quiet. She always busies herself with a book. Whether she reads or not, he doesn't know. She's cold to him, and her behaviour makes him angry. Since he told her Hanna's story, she has changed. She has a stinging tongue filled with sarcastic words. He can't bear her ignoring him. He told her he's not ready yet to adopt a child. He never will be. Any child reminds him of Hanna's daughter. Hanna's daughter!

He brings out the bottle of whisky. Afsaneh eyes him indifferently, saying nothing.

"Would you like me to pour a glass for you too?"

She nods her head, no. He fills his glass half-full. Before touching his food, he empties his glass. His stomach burns. She lifts her head from her book and watches him, disapprovingly.

"What is it? Why are you looking at me?"

She doesn't answer. She puts a little food on her plate. She has cooked rice mixed with green beans. No more fancy dinners, with candles, a bottle of wine, long stem glasses by each plate and roses or carnations. She's lost her enthusiasm, but he's still happy with her. Those luxuries were too much for him. He needs only Afsaneh. He wants her, but her presence brings pain now, sweet pain. He still wants her. He's like a cancer patient enduring a terrible pain and still wanting to live. Anything that will lengthen the days of his life. Sometimes her behaviour forces him to get drunk, to forget. He realizes Afsaneh has changed. Love is gone. She pushes him away, doesn't want to sleep with him, or if she does, she's like stone. She stays away from him. Why doesn't she leave him? She may still love him. She doesn't know him yet. If she knows him as he is... He hasn't told her that when Behnaz drowned, he was glad. He hasn't told her that his cry was one of pure joy. He hasn't told her that he stayed on the shore until he was sure Behnaz had been taken by the wave. Then he went to the villa and pretended he didn't know where Behnaz was. If she heard this, she would leave him tonight. He looks at her. Why doesn't she say anything? She doesn't talk about the city, about the Quebecois, who speak French like people in the North of Iran speak Farsi, with a special accent. Why is she so bitter? Because of what he said about Hanna or because he can't give her a baby? They stare at each other for a while.

"Why are you upset?" he asks.

She doesn't answer.

"A little alcohol isn't bad," he says, "if you don't like whisky, I'll bring you wine."

"You need it, not me."

Anger flares up in his body. He fills his glass and empties it. His voice breaks. "Obviously I need it. When you're so cold."

She looks at him indifferently, and then pushes her chair away. Her food is half-eaten. Taking her book from the table, she strolls to the library, the room where she spends most of her time. She closes the door. He's fuming, wondering what to do. He swallows a few more gulps of whisky and opens the door. She's squatting on a sofa. He stands in front of her. His throat and stomach are burning. He's hot and damp with sweat.

"What happened?" he asks, "why can't you forgive me? Do you think I'm a murderer?"

She looks at him, stunned, fear in her eyes. She stays quiet.

"What have I done to you? Why have you changed?"

"Leave me alone. I'm fed up."

"I know why you're fed up. You want a baby. I can't give it to you. This is something I can't do. You must understand. I didn't do it for myself. I felt I was guilty. Do you understand that? I am guilty. I have suffered."

And suddenly a scream bursts in him, and he can't control himself. Another Bahram is growing in him, speaks for him. He breaks the silence of years. "Listen. There are still many things I haven't told you. Can you stand to hear the rest of it?"

"You're drunk," she says, "go and get some cold water."

"I'm not drunk. I'm more conscious. I'm a murderer. A murderer, do you understand?"

He sits by Afsaneh's feet on the floor. His head is heavy. His voice breaks, but the words are flowing out and he can't stop them. He knows these words will ruin his life, but he has to speak. They're a lump burdening his chest. Behnaz is in front of him, standing in the water, making fun of him, calling him a chicken, laughing at him, and throwing herself into the water, moving her hands and legs. A big wave rushes to the shore. As if the wave is his anger, coming to take Behnaz away. He can call Behnaz, and tell her about the wave. He stays quiet. The wave passes over his head too, but he runs to the shore. The wave passes, and he's on the shore, but Behnaz isn't. He knows the wave has taken her into the sea. He waits, and then he goes back to the villa.

"Don't look at me like that. I told you about Behnaz, but it wasn't the whole story. I drowned her. I knew a big wave swept her into the sea, but I stayed on the shore to be sure she wouldn't be back. Then I went to the villa."

Afsaneh says nothing. Looks at him, unbelieving. The book in her hand is open. He feels sorry for Afsaneh, but he can't stop himself speaking.

"I'm not finished yet. Do you know the story of Mahmood?"

"The one who committed suicide, who worked in our old office in Tehran?" she mumbles.

"Yes, the one who threw himself from the sixth floor. I forced him to kill himself. I took the bribe, but he was caught. I fled the country in time. Do you understand? I know how to escape in time."

She's dumbfounded, saying, "Don't lie. You're drunk."

"I'm not drunk. Believe me, I'm not."

"You said you had to go Montreal on urgent business, to be with the consulting engineers. Did you lie to me? And because of that, you didn't want me to talk about Mahmood? So you..." She stops talking.

He wants her to speak more, to reproach him, but Afsaneh just looks at him with embarrassment. What he has said convinces him to say everything. Afsaneh's curiosity makes him say more.

"And Hanna, I pushed Hanna to kill herself. I could have kept her hopeful. I could have gone to her after my father left. But when he left and two weeks later I heard that he had died, I couldn't go to her. Not because of my father. I didn't want to go. I could have gone to her even when my father was here. I could have kept my promise to Hanna, but I didn't. I took Father's letter with the cheque. She saw the cheque and her eyes were full of hurt, like Behnaz's face. And I got rid of her. You see Afsaneh, I'm a murderer. There's another Bahram in me who leads me, decides for me. Afsaneh, help me get rid of this Bahram. I need your help."

He sees fear clearly in Afsaneh's eyes. She holds her tongue. She wants to get up and leave. Escape. He grabs her hand, bursting into sobs. He's finally relaxed, he has revealed himself fully to Afsaneh. He expects Afsaneh to sympathize with him, as she did when he told Behnaz's story. Soothe him, say it wasn't his fault. He wants her to say, kill that Bahram in yourself and throw him away. You can be a new man. She says nothing. Her eyes are full of fear.

"Don't be so hard on me," he says, "help me. Don't leave me. Please stay with me."

Afsaneh's look mortifies him. He stretches his hand out to her, she pushes it back. He comes closer to her, wants to hug her, lay his head on her chest. She pushes him back in silence. There's loathing in her eyes. He's screaming inside, don't be disgusted with me. He has been truthful. He has confessed everything. Afsaneh shows no reaction. She doesn't soothe him. He begs her, "Afsaneh don't be so hard on me."

Afsaneh is still quiet. Anger flares up in him. He pulls her to him, kisses her roughly. She tries to pull away, but he doesn't let her. He puts his hand in her dress collar and presses her breasts hard, tearing her dress off. Afsaneh screams in rage and pain, pulling away abruptly, and kicks him. She leaves the room. He regrets what he has done. Afsaneh may leave him. Crumpling to the floor, he hears the apartment door open and close with a bang. She has left. He rushes onto the balcony, sees her leaving the building. "Afsaneh," he screams.

His voice disappears into the silence of the fall night. The wind blows last night's snow from the roofs onto his face. Looking down, he feels dizzy. He's tempted to climb the railing and jump. A gust of cold air pushes him into the apartment.

"I'm talking about Mahmood. The one whose wife recently had a baby, and we went to the hospital to visit her. He jumped out of their apartment window, from the sixth floor, and was killed instantly. His brain spattered onto the pavement. They said he bribed someone. I can't believe it."

"Afsaneh, leave this for later on. Talk about yourself. When are you going to come?"

"I have a visa to France. Next week I go to Paris, then to Toulouse. I want to stay in France a few days. My uncle is sick. He doesn't work any more. I want to see him. Ida has two daughters, and Majid Khan said she's pregnant again. Ida is two years older than me, and her older daughter is eight years old. Ida has an Iranian husband, and her older daughter is called Shahrazad, the younger is Louise or Liz, I don't know. Majid Khan told me, but I forget. I'd like to see her daughters. They're my relatives. And me, I want to have a daughter."

"Afsaneh, think of the cost of long distance calls. You can tell me these things when you get here."

"I want two daughters and a son. I like girls more. I'll call them…

"Afsaneh, let's leave dreaming for another time."

"I'll call one of my daughters, Firoozeh, in memory of

Firoozeh, and the other one, I'll call her Sara, in memory of my mother. Or Behnaz. Yes, I'll call her Behnaz, in memory of your little sister."

"Afsaneh, what happened to you? Are you crazy? Are you crazy because you're far away from me?"

"I'm happy, that's all."

The moon has disappeared. It's close to dawn, and Bahram is still wandering by the lake. He was with Afsaneh the whole night. Hearing Afsaneh's voice. He hears her now, too. He can't see her, but he knows she's there. Somewhere around here. Where's here? He doesn't know. He hears her voice. All night he and Afsaneh talked.

"Come on. Don't be afraid. Don't let me call you a chicken. The water is warm. Come closer. Here…"

He hears Afsaneh laughing loudly and follows the laughter. Where? He doesn't know. Somewhere faraway, somewhere without any Behnaz, Hanna, or Mahmood. There's only Afsaneh, and water. Afsaneh, moon, and earth. Afsaneh and trees.

The sun is rising and the lake is waking under golden rays of sunrise. A motor boat is shrieking, tearing apart the silence. The lake wrinkles and waves comes closer. Bahram regains himself. His elation is gone, a new day is stretching ahead of him, but he still hears Afsaneh reciting,

More pleasant than the sound of love's speech, naught heard
A great keepsake that in this revolving dome remained.

Born in Hamadan, Iran, Mehri Yalfani began writing short stories in high school. Her first collection of stories, *Happy Days*, was published in 1966. After finishing high school, she moved to Tehran to study and graduated from the University of Tehran in electrical engineering. She worked as an engineer for the next twenty years, raising three children and working full time. Her second book, the novel, *Before the Fall*, was published in Iran in 1980.

In 1985, Mehri Yalfani immigrated to France and then, in 1987, to Canada with her family. Since then she has published in many Farsi and English-language publications. Two collections of short stories and three novels in Farsi have been published in Sweden, USA and Canada. Her most recent Farsi novel, *Dancing In A Broken Mirror*, was published in Iran. Two collections of short stories in English — *Parastoo* and *Two Sisters* — have been published in Canada, by Women's Press and TSAR.

Mehri Yalfani lives in Toronto.